MW00967541

That's My Testimony

Written By
Annetta Swift

Printed in Victoria, Canada

National Library of Canada Cataloguing in Publication

Swift, Annetta, 1971-
...That's my testimony / Annetta Swift.

ISBN 1-4120-0263-X

    I. Title.

PS3619.W447T43 2003   813'.6   C2003-902345-1

This book was published *on-demand* in cooperation with Trafford Publishing.
On-demand publishing is a unique process and service of making a book available for retail sale to the public taking advantage of on-demand manufacturing and Internet marketing.
On-demand publishing includes promotions, retail sales, manufacturing, order fulfilment, accounting and collecting royalties on behalf of the author.

Suite 6E, 2333 Government St., Victoria, B.C. V8T 4P4, CANADA
Phone   250-383-6864   Toll-free   1-888-232-4444 (Canada & US)
Fax   250-383-6804   E-mail   sales@trafford.com
Web site   www.trafford.com   TRAFFORD PUBLISHING IS A DIVISION OF TRAFFORD HOLDINGS LTD.
Trafford Catalogue #03-0632   www.trafford.com/robots/03-0632.html

10   9   8   7   6   5   4   3   2   1

Special Thanks To:

My Lord and Savior, Jesus Christ, He's the only reason that I can do all things. Without him I am nothing.

To my darling husband, Rodney Swift, thanks for letting me burn the midnight oil. Your faith in me has kept me going throughout this project. Thanks for your encouragement and your unselfishness.

To my baby, Syrinthia Swift, thanks for understanding that "Mommy is busy." Now we will have plenty of "Barbie Time".

To Universal Outreach Ministries, for believing in me enough to sponsor this project and have it published. The harvest from this seed will return not many days hence.

To my mom and dad, John and Gloria Coates, I appreciate you bringing me up in the fear and admonition of the Lord. If it wasn't for my past, I couldn't stand in the present and walk toward my future.

To Mom and Dad Swift, thanks for your constant support.

To my brother, Reginald "Red" Swift, I'm coming out and I am bringing you with me. Thanks for your input.

To Lina "Pat" Watts, thanks for the background information and research.

To Phyllis, my best friend, my sounding board, and fan club, thanks for all of the hours you unselfishly gave. God will reward you greatly.

To Marilyn, my oldest sister thanks for your confidence in me. It means a lot.

To Rhonda Moore and Regina Swift, my little sisters, you're always there when I need you. Thanks.

To Tara D. Upshaw, thanks for the hook up.

To Apostle Belle, Elder Charles Milliner, Pastor Christine Lewis, and Nutrix Ministries my spiritual mentors, thanks for believing in me.

To Prophet Troy Sanders, thanks for releasing the gift in me and speaking this into existence. Continue to let God use you.

To Reina Redwine, my spiritual twin, thanks for all of the time you spent proofreading and making corrections on this project. It is proof positive that you are a true friend.

To Sharonne Thomas and Gia Browder, for the sweat and tears you put into making sure that the book was "reader ready" by the deadlines. Your work was not in vain.

To La-shun Turner and Chareisse Larke I love you dearly.

Finally, to all my friends and family, far too many to name on this page alone, thank you for your prayers and support.

INTRODUCTION

Women have many issues to deal with in life, most of which they don't share. There are some experiences too shameful to mention even to one's own conscience. That is why this book was written -- to tell the story of the lives of these women. Although the characters are fictional, their stories are real. This work is a compilation of different people's lives. Each reader will see herself in one or more of these women. Not only do the characters expose intimate details of their lives in all of its gore and heartache, they show how these situations that should've taken their sanity, brought them to know God in a real way. These women are survivors and have determined in their hearts and minds that they will fulfill the purpose of God in their lives. They have grabbed hold of destiny and are ready to tell you their TESTIMONIES...

That's My Testimony

By Annetta Swift

Chapter One

ANGEL

Looking back it seems as if it were yesterday. There I was an 18-year-old high school graduate getting ready to move across the country for college. Perhaps FAMU would have been ideal for me, but I had to escape my parents' jail. All we ever did was attend church. It was so frustrating being on a ball and chain. Pants were forbidden, make-up was a no-no, and extra curricular activities were out of the question. The biggest sins were the going to the movies and dating. In school, no one even knew that I was a prisoner of religion. Living two lives was never easy, so I vowed that once I graduated, I was moving far away from my parents and God. In autumn of that year, I enrolled at Washington State University in Pullman, Washington.

"FREE AT LAST, THANK GOD ALMIGHTY, I AM FREE!" I exclaimed, as I dropped my bags down in the middle of my dorm room floor. "Woo!" Bliss and joy overshadowed my soul. It didn't even make a difference who my roommate would be since freedom was my new best friend.

My roommate's name was LaKeesha Bedford, and we instantly became close.

She was from a little town about three hours away from Seattle. We had very little in common except for the fact that we loved having a good time. I was raised in church and she rarely went to church. My parents had me on lock and key, she was brought up in a single parent home with the freedom of an adult. Despite our differences, we ended up kicking it and hanging out all of the time. It wasn't long after school started that guys were coming out of the woodwork, but no one interested me the way Demetrius Long did. He was so fine. His complexion was pecan tan. He had the prettiest skin, teeth and hair -- he was a bag of chips and a coke. Although beauty wasn't my number one feature, it never stopped men from approaching me. I was about 5'4" and about 125 pounds with a mocha bronze shell. There was no comparison to my roommate and me. She was very pretty with the perfect figure and she also had the personality to match. During winter break, Keesha invited me to go home with her, but my plans only consisted of seeing all of Demetrius. He was my first. One thing my parents had drilled in me was to "wait until you were married to have sex". Even with all of my restraint, I couldn't resist him. His game was just as smooth as his lips. He ha d his own place, was a senior, a football player and had a 3.2 grade point average. He was not too far from perfect in my mind. By spring break, we were roommates and it seemed like a dream come true. With all of this freedom and fun, there was no way my parents would see me until summer vacation. My parents were really concerned, but once they heard my voice they were fine. My dad told me that my mom was in and out of the hospital. She had been most of my life, so I didn't think much of it. By the end of my freshman year, my interest peaked in hairstyling. It was hard to drop out of college, but I wasn't fulfilled there. I enrolled at Washington School of Cosmetology. It was in the heart of downtown Seattle, and only a few minutes away from where Demetrius and I lived. Metchie (that's what they called him.) graduated *CUM LAUDE,* with a bachelor's in education. Although he was a great football player, his goal was to be a teacher. In the fall he was going to continue on at Washington State to get his Master's degree.

"Well, are you ready to go home?" Metchie asked me.

"Yeah. I guess. I haven't seen my parents in almost a year, and my mom is back in the hospital, so I think it's about that time. My dad sent my ticket about a week ago. He is really excited. I just hope they don't start that 'you need to be saved' stuff."

"I never had any bad church experiences like you have but I can understand how you feel," he said.

"I don't know how I am going to survive being away from you all this time," I answered sadly.

"Two weeks is a long time, but we'll talk everyday," he promised.

"Well, when I get back we gone have to make up for lost time."

"That just makes it MO BETTA!" we both laughed.

"Here, this is a little something I got you but don't read it until you're either on the plane or in Florida." He handed me an envelope.

"O.k. Thank you."

Metchie was born and raised in Seattle, so he was home. He was going to go to summer school just to get ahead of the game but he felt that he would just do some over time at his job. He was a teller at the 1st Community Bank and had that job since he was a freshman in college. He always had money in his pockets, receiving his check from the bank along with his stipend from his scholarship. He wouldn't let me have a summer job and we hardly ever ate in. As a matter of fact, the envelope he gave me was a love note and $200 in cash. I really thought I was in love.

As the plane landed nausea overcame me. Fear of the drama that would possibly be awaiting me made me sick. My dad was not at the gate to greet me as I expected. He was usually late. I went on to the baggage claim

area, and I heard my name being
hollered.

"Angel! Angel!" My dad shouted.
I turned around and ran to hug him. He
looked as if he had seen a ghost. He
has never seen me in pants, or make up,
and I had two holes in each of my ears.
Of course my hair was laid, and I had
a honey blonde rinse in it. "Hey
daddy! I am so glad to see you. You
really look good."

"I wish I could say the same. How can
you come here looking like a Jezebel?"

"What! I mean can't I get off of the
plane good before you start preaching
to me. We haven't seen each other in
almost a year, and you couldn't say
anything nice to me."

"We'll talk in the car."

Man, I didn't come home for this.
I thought, "Why can't I live my own
life? They chose to be holier than
thou, not me. I guess they're going to
have a complete cardiac arrest when I
tell them I am going to beauty school.
They just may drop dead when I tell
them I am living with my man. I may
have to keep that bit of information to
myself. Seeing how whenever I call I
am at Keesha's dorm room. Maybe I can
tell them that Keesha and I have an
apartment. How would I explain paying
rent with no job? I'll cross that
bridge when I get to it."

"Girl, what have you been doing out there? You done forgot everything we taught you about holiness." He said.
I just continued to stare out of the window.
"Don't you hear me talking to you?" He said.
"Yes."
"We're going to the house first, so that you can change before your mom sees you like that."
"Like what?"
"You know. Face all painted up, hair all colored up, holes all in your ears. What's wrong with you? You done lost your mind or what?"
"No sir. I actually thought that it wouldn't matter. I just thought that you would be happy to see me. I am sorry I am such a disappointment to you," I stated.
"Well, I am very disappointed, and we ain't gone disappoint your mother. So when we get to the house I expect you to change into a dress, and wash that paint off of your face. Your mom is sick enough. She don't need this."
"Yes sir."

The rest of the ride was silent. When we got home I did as he ordered. I put on my jean skirt, a tee shirt, sox and tennis shoes, and I washed my face. I looked a hot mess. Mom looked bad. She was happy to see me, but she was really sick. She had breast cancer and had been undergoing chemotherapy, and all her hair is gone. If they are

so religious, why won't God heal mom?
I didn't understand. I did eventually
tell dad that I dropped out of college
to go to cosmetology school. He
actually took that well. I've always
been an honest person, so I even told
him about Metchie and me. Dad blew up.
He sentenced me to hell, and told me
until I got my life right that I
couldn't bring damnation on his house.
So my two-week trip turned into three
days of hell. Metchie picked me up
from the airport. I thought we would
spend all night making love, but I
ended up crying the whole night.

Metchie and I kicked for the next
few years. I got my license and began
working at a popular hair salon. I
would call home periodically, and my
dad was cold and short. Mom had
sympathy in her voice but she didn't
say much to me about anything. She was
doing well and has begun to grow hair
again. I was still not allowed in
their home. I guess if we ever decided
to get married, they would not come.
It really hurts, but over the years I
had learned to cope with it. LaKeesha
was pregnant and expecting a boy. She
had some major complications at first,
but they progressed well. Keesha's
man's name was Phil. She doesn't live
with him, though.

She always said, "Girl, I ain't
living with no man unless he is my
husband. You can do what you like but
those are my rules."

I respected her for that and we
agreed to disagree on that matter. I
didn't see much difference in what
either one of us was doing. I was
living in the restaurant, and she was
going through the pick up window. We
both were eating fast food, which isn't
healthy either way. Oh, well.

Things started to get a little
tense with Metchie and I. He started
coming home late, and doing weird stuff
like sleeping on the couch. He was
getting strange phone calls, and he
wasn't trying to be intimate with me at
all, not even kissing. When I would
get home from work some nights, he
wouldn't even be home. I'd ask him
what was up, but he would say I
wouldn't understand. What I did
understand is that this man must have
bumped his head. I am not going to sit
around and let nobody play me in my
face. "Oh, No!" I guess I am going to
have to let Romeo go. One night when
he came in I went off.
"Where you been?" I yelled.

He just kept on walking with his
head down.

"Hey, I know you hear me!"

He went into the bathroom and ran
the shower as if I wasn't even there.

"Metchie, you are so low down. How
can you do this to me? I have been
nothing but good to you."
"Look, let me get a shower and then
I'll explain everything. O.k.?"

The thing that made me so mad is that he was so calm. How could someone be so low? After his shower, he took me by the hand and led me to the couch. "Sit down." He said.

I did.

"There has been a lot of things that I have been dealing with lately, and I've been so hesitant to come to you, but I knew that it would have to be soon. I have not been seeing other women. Well, not in the form of cheating. This girl I met named Tracy invited me to go to church with her. I didn't ask you because I already knew how you felt about God and religion. The thing is, I only intended on going once. When I got there it felt so good. The singing was the bomb. The thing that blew my mind was this preacher that I never knew, knew me and read me like a book. Almost like a psychic, but I could feel him and he felt me. It was like metal being drawn to a magnet. I started going every Wednesday night and Friday night. What I am saying in a nutshell is that I gave my life over to Christ. I knew that we couldn't do it no more and eventually either you or me would have to move. Tracy is married, and it was no happenings there. I made a choice to serve God and I can't have peace until one of us moves."

"Wait a minute. You're saved?"

"Girl, yes. Sanctified and Holy Ghost filled." He said, smiling. "Angel, I

wish you would come with me. It is
nothing like the church you grew up in.
This is the best feeling I've ever had.
I just can't deal with the guilt of not
pleasing God, living with you. Even
though ain't nothing happening..."
"You've got that right."
" I know we can't go on like this and
not be married"
"I am only 21. I am not ready to be
married, Metch."
"We would have to go through counseling
any way. So either way it goes, one of
us has to move. I've been giving this
a lot of thought and I have decided to
move. I'll sacrifice and help you
financially all I can until you find
another place or a roommate." He
reached for my hand.

I jerked my hand away. "I don't
believe this. Metchie, I would never
ask you to give up your place. You
have so much invested in it. I know
that I could probably stay with Keesha
until I got on my feet. I'll just talk
to her tomorrow. She felt like I was
going to end up staying with her
anyway. Only difference is that she
thought it would be because of another
woman, not God. Maybe my parents cursed
me..."

"Un, uh! Don't even go there. My
being saved is no curse. This is a
blessing."

"For who?"
"For me. It could be for you to if you
would except it."

"I don't want it. I want you, Metchie."

"You can have me, just not like this. It has to be on God's terms."
He reached to hug me.

"Don't touch me. What am I supposed to do? I can't get over you overnight. You were the first guy I fell in love with and the first guy I ever had sex with. We have invested years into this relationship and you are willing to let it go over church?"

"Angel, it is not that simple for me. Don't you know how much I love you? This is hurting me too, but I can't choose you over God. I'll get over this hurt. There is no way that I can live without Him."

"Is that all?"

"There's really not much more I can say. The ball is in your court now," He said, with tears in his eyes.

"Well, I'll make it easy for you. I'll pack my things and head over to Keesha's. Whatever I don't get tonight, I'll pick up later," I said.

He nodded. I was relieved that it wasn't anybody else, but the fact still remained that it was over.

I drove on over to Keesha's, hoping that she would still be awake. She used to be a nighthawk but since she's been pregnant she is always in hibernation. As I approached the apartment I noticed that the television was on. I had to knock at least 3 times before she even responded.

"Yes, who is it?" She said. She was
very pleasant, seeing that it was 1:47
a.m.

"It's me, Angel."

She opened the door. She swiftly
ran to the lamp to turn on the light.

"Girl, what happened?"

"You were right. Well, partially.
There are no other women…"

"Girl, is he gay?"

"No, Keesha. Just listen. He is a
born again Christian girl."

"Girl, no. Like your mom and
dad!"

"Yes and no. His church is
nothing like the one I grew up in. He
actually wants me to be a part of it
with him. He says we can no longer
live in sin. That's why we haven't
been doing anything and he's been on
the couch. In order for us to remain a
couple we have to get counseling and
then get married. I am not ready for
all of that. So I am giving him his
space. It hurts so much." I broke down
in tears.

Keesha grabbed me and hugged me.
"Well, if you need some place to stay
you know you can stay here."

"I know. I appreciate it. I know
that you are not Metchie and I will pay
you whatever you say."

"Girl, we have plenty of time to
discuss all of that. Just go in the
other room and get you some rest. What
time is your first client in the
morning?"

"Not until ten."

"We'll talk in the morning."

I don't know if I even went to sleep. I believe I cried all night long. As the days went on, it got easier to handle. My parents were thrilled about my misfortune. The next couple of weeks my days seemed a big blur. I wasn't eating as a matter of fact I lost 5 or 10 pounds. Business at the salon was slow and I just wanted to die. I didn't think that matters could get any worse, but when it rains it pours. I didn't expect more rain.

"RING... RING..."

"I guess I'll get it. Good morning, Simply Elegance Hair Salon, this is Angel. How may I help you?" "Angel. Hey this is Phil."

My heart dropped. I knew something was up. He has never called me and for him to call my job really scared me. "What's wrong?"

"It's Keesha. She went into labor and..."

"Where are y'all?"

"We're at St. John's Medical Center in the emergency room. They are trying to stop the labor. She is seven months..." He broke down.

"Look, Phil, you have to be strong for her. With all of the modern technology I am sure everything will be all right. I'm going to see if Deidra will cover my next client for me and I'll be right there."

"O. K."

"Deidra can you come here for a minute?"

"What's up, girl?"

I explained the situation and she immediately agreed to take my client. I called my client on her cell phone and she had no problem going to Deidra. As I drove so many thoughts were going through my mind. There were thoughts of Metchie, my family in Florida and Keesha. All of a sudden this scene flashed before my face. I could see myself walking slowly up this aisle. As I held my head up, I saw a casket. I was trying to see who it was, but by the time I reached the casket the picture left. I was overcome by grief. I couldn't stop crying. I didn't know if it was my mother or me being paranoid.

When I arrived at the hospital, I had to get myself together. I looked in the mirror and I looked like death. I put on some make-up and went in. It was almost like a reunion. There was Phil, his mom, Keesha's mom and grandma. Even Keesha's deadbeat dad was there. Although Keesha and I were best friends, we were more like sisters. Everyone thought we were anyway. Even her family had adopted me.

"Ma. How is she?" I asked.

"Baby, I really don't know. They couldn't stop her contractions and the baby was getting distressed so they had to rush her into surgery. We just have to pray that she and the baby are all right."

We held hands and waited what seemed to be an eternity when the doctor came in and dropped the bomb.

"Is she all right? How's the baby?" Ma asked.

"Mrs. Bedford I am sorry," the doctor said. "We tried all we could, but the baby didn't make it."

There went Ma and Phil falling out on the floor. Grandma ran to grab Ma, and Phil's mom had him. I walked to the doctor.

"What happened?" I asked.

"Well, frankly, the baby's lungs were underdeveloped and when we went to take the baby out, the umbilical cord was wrapped around his neck. Once we removed it, the staff did all they could but the little fellow wouldn't breathe."

"How is Keesha?" I asked.

"Well, she's going to be fine. She is still in recovery. From there she'll be in ICU. She has no idea of what has happened, so the next hurdle will be telling her she lost her baby," He said.

I fell in his arms and wailed. He comforted me as only a doctor could. I could tell he was concerned but it wasn't the same as if a loved one comforted you. It was fine for that moment.

In the intensive care unit only two people are allowed in at a time. Phil

let me and Ma go in first. He said he
couldn't bear the thought of seeing her
once she initially heard what had
happened. Ma and I were in the room
once the anesthesia started to wear
off. She opened her eyes.

"Hey, baby." Ma said rubbing her
hand.

It was so hard for me not to cry.
Knowing what we had to tell her and
then seeing her hooked up to all of
these monitors and tubes up her nose I
felt like dying. Keesha's voice was so
soft and weak.

"Ma. How's the baby? Is the baby
ok?" She asked.
Ma cleared her throat. "Keesha they
had some complications, honey. Um…
well…"

"What? What? Please, how is the
baby?" she asked looking at me.

"What Ma is trying to tell you
is…"

"Dog gone it WHAT?" she asked
hoarsely.

"The baby didn't make it," I said.

"Didn't make what?"

"He's dead Keesha," Ma said.

"NO! NO! NO! … OH MY GOD! NO!
WHY? WHAT HAPPENED?"

She yelled and cried. The nurse
came in. Keesha was going off. Ma and
the nurse were trying to keep her calm
and still, but the more they restrained
her the more she fought to get loose.

"I WANNA SEE MY BABY. WHERE IS MY
BABY?" She kept saying over and over.

I had to leave out. I couldn't bear to
see my sister, my ace, break down like
this. Through all of the excitement
Keesha started bleeding very heavily.
The nurses were trying to find where
the blood was coming from. They told
Ma she had to get out. They ended up
having to take her back to surgery so
that they could find the source of
bleeding and stop it before she would
hemorrhage to death.

By this time we were all bugging
out. The staff finally got us to calm
down a little. The next few hours
brought about so many different
thoughts. For one, what was taking
them so long? Then I wondered how the
heck was I going to handle going to the
apartment alone and looking at all of
that baby stuff? I knew that I would
have to get it out of the apartment
before Keesha got home. Once I saw the
doctor's expression as he came to the
waiting room, I knew the news was not
good. His face was red and he was
constantly rubbing his hands while he
was talking.

"I am sorry. Lakeesha began to
hemorrhage as we were opening her and
while on the operating table her heart
rate plummeted and suddenly she flat-
lined."

His voice was trembling. I'd
jumped up before I knew it and grabbed
him.

"What have you done? What
happened? Don't you say it! No! No!"
I screamed.

The room that day was full of
chaos. Keesha was gone, dead. Why not
me? She didn't deserve this. I felt
like I was in a nightmare. Did God
hate me so much that He would take away
all that I loved? I remembered the
story of Job in the Bible, but he was a
good guy -- I was nothing but a curse.
Everything and everyone that knew me
needed not be around because I was a
bad luck charm. I just got up and
left. I had done enough damage for the
day. I got in my car and began
driving. I didn't know where to go. I
couldn't go home. We shared the same
house. I thought, maybe I'll just
drive off of a cliff or take an
overdose of pills. Yeah. I still had
my prescription for anti-depressants in
my purse that my doctor gave me a few
weeks ago when Metchie and I broke up.
I'll just go get them from the drug
store and end all of this drama. As I
drove, I couldn't even see for my
tears. The next thing I knew here
comes this police officer pulling me
over. What in the world did I do so
bad that made God hate me so? He
tapped on the window. I rolled it
down.

"Ma'am do you know why I stopped
you?" he asked.

"Because I am cursed, perhaps. I
don't know."

"Um... well, let me have your license and registration. You failed to stop at two traffic lights, ma'am. You could've created a terrible situation if there were other cars coming."

He took my information, and went back to his car. He came back and handed me my stuff, and I set it on the seat next to me.

"Where are you headed?" he asked.

"To the drug store."

"Do you need me to escort you there?"

"No. I'll be fine."

"Ma'am please be careful."

"O.k.," I said rolling up my window.

The drug store was only a block or so away. As I parked, I grabbed my purse to look for the prescription and I realized that I never signed my ticket. I picked up my license and registration and what looked like a brochure. I read, "When all else fails, Try Jesus." Was God really trying to tell me something? I opened it and the officer had stuck a little note in there that said, "I don't know what you're dealing with, but Christ is the only way out." It was as if he knew that I was going to kill myself. On the back of the brochure was the address to a church with the order of service. I figured I had never given God a chance and things couldn't get much worse. I decided I'd go Sunday,

and if God didn't prove Himself to be
real then I would leave church and kill
myself. I was still going to get my
prescription filled just in case.

   We had a double funeral for
Lakeesha Dayshon Bedford and Phillip
Lemar Johnson, Jr. This was the
saddest funeral that I had ever
attended. One Friday I bury my best
friend and godson. The next Friday
maybe they'd be burying me. I decided
to go to church on Sunday and hoped
something would happen to change my
life because I really didn't want to
kill myself, but I thought I really
didn't have anything else to live for.

   As I stepped in the church I felt
chills going up and down my spine.
There were two ushers there to greet
me. I couldn't believe it. I was in a
holiness church and the usher had on
earrings and make-up, but she looked
nice. They seated me and gave me some
papers to fill out. I felt like a
total heathen. I was raised in the
church and there I was with no Bible.
All I had in my hand was the brochure
that I got from the officer. I had no
recollection of how he looked. I
wouldn't know him if he slapped me in
the face. "Oh well," I thought, maybe
he'll recognize me." As the service
started, the music began playing. It
was so pretty. I just started crying.
I think I cried through the entire
devotional service. During the time
that they recognized visitors they gave

space for anyone to have words. I
don't know why, but I stood up, they
handed me a microphone, and I spoke.

"Hi. My name is Angel Butler. I
am originally from Jacksonville,
Florida. I was raised in the church,
but my parents beat me over the head
with religion, and once I graduated
from high school I moved here. Three
years ago my parents disassociated
themselves from me because I was living
in sin with my boyfriend. They said
that I would bring damnation on them.
So all I had were my friends here.
About a month ago my boyfriend broke up
with me so I moved out of his place and
in with my best friend. Last week, we
buried my best friend and her son. I
felt I had nothing to live for, but the
day my friend and her son died I was
pulled over by a police officer - I was
on my way to commit suicide. Instead
of the officer giving me the ticket
that I deserved, he handed me this
brochure." I lifted it to show the
congregation.

"Inside he wrote me a note that
said 'Jesus is the only way out'. I
began to think what if God is real?
What if hell is real? I knew that I
had never given God a chance and this
was my last hope. On the back was the
address here. I said if this doesn't
work, after service I am going to end
it all."

I broke down in tears. The
minister came down and embraced me.

This was unheard of at my church back home. The men only shook hands with the women. It was different but it felt right. I felt so much love from this man, almost like he was my daddy. He called the ministers over to pray for me. They actually had women ministers. Wow. They told me to lift my hands and they began to pray. I heard them casting demonic spirits off of me. They were telling the devil to release me and to come out of me like I was the in the exorcist or something. Then I began to gag. This clear stuff was coming out of my mouth. I was so scared. They had this towel around me, and they were saying, "there it is." I'm thinking there what is? After I threw up all that stuff they began to tell me to say thank you, Jesus. I did just what they said. I said it over and over until I wasn't saying it any more. I was speaking in another tongue. I heard other people do it when I was younger, but I didn't think that it was real. Everyone made it seem so mystical but it wasn't. I didn't see any lights and nothing picked me up. I was just praising my God. All of those negative thoughts and emotions were gone. I felt like I had taken a nice hot bath after playing in the dirt. I was so refreshed. The minister asked me to say how I felt but when I attempted to speak no English came out, only another language. Everyone including me started jumping and

praising God. God is really real. At
the end of the service everyone was
hugging me. The minister never got a
chance to do his sermon. I had never
experienced such freedom in church. I
was so glad I had decided to come. The
officer didn't put his name on the
brochure so I didn't know whom to ask
for. The congregation was rather large
with 100 people or so, but small enough
for someone to know him. In the midst
of all of the hugs there was a tap on
my shoulder. I almost fainted. It was
Metchie.

"Oh my God, girl. I can't believe
this. I knew that God answered
prayers, but who would've thought He
would answer this quick."

"This is the church that you've
been going to?"

"Yes. Girl, I am so happy right
now. I am sorry about Keesha and all.
I saw you at the funeral, but I didn't
want to impose on you guys."

"I understand."

I reached for him to hug him. We
embraced and cried, and embraced and
cried again. It was beautiful. God
was truly awesome. I stayed in
Keesha's apartment until her lease was
up and then I moved in with her mom.
As destiny would have it, Metchie and I
went through counseling and were
married. We both became very active in
our church and began growing daily in
the Lord. My parents and I renewed our
relationship. Dad has mellowed out a

whole lot. God healed my mother and she has no trace of cancer. The most ironic thing about this situation is that the minister was the officer that gave me the brochure. Yes, God is real. If I could change my life I would've worked things out a little differently. Now I'll just take my experiences and learn from them. I am now Angel Long, hairstylist, wife, and most importantly, woman of God. I may never stand behind a podium and take a text, but I surely have a testimony.

Chapter Two

DENISE

I have always been a loner, but at the same time, I've always wanted to fit in. Ever since I can remember I have always tried to be something that everyone else wanted me to be. The more I tried, the more people wanted out of me. I grew up in the house with my brother, my grandfather, my aunt, and her three kids. My brother's name is Dennis. We weren't twins, but we were 15 months apart. I am the oldest. My dad killed my mom when I was a baby and he is in prison. I've never gone to see him. I haven't had a desire to see the man that is responsible for leaving me motherless. I know that there are two sides to every story, but his side doesn't even matter to me. From what I have heard, my parents were always arguing and the last one was the last one. As fate would have it, we had no choice of who we'd stay with. My grandfather adopted us, and my aunt moved in with him to help -- so she says. I've always wondered what happened in my life to make me the type of person I am. I was so needy of people's attention, but yet too shy to go around others. Perhaps it came from being rejected and mistreated so much

as a child. I can remember as if it
were yesterday -- Christmas of 1969. I
was five years old with my cousins and
my brother. We found the place where
the toys were hidden. We never
believed in Santa Clause, but we always
had big holidays with our entire
family.

"Oooo wee!" I exclaimed. "I can't
wait to play with that baby doll. She
looks so real."

"Yep. She does," my cousin Leslie
agreed. She and I were the only girls
in the house and there were baby dolls,
Barbie dolls, skates, and a great big
dollhouse. We had already decided
which one of us would get each baby and
we both would share the dollhouse.
Leslie was seven years old and had a
nine-year old brother named Damond and
a five-year old brother, Leon.   The
boys got a racetrack and too many
trucks to count. We heard Auntie Bib
coming. Everyone called her Bib
because my uncle couldn't say Vivian
when they were kids so it just carried
on.

"What are y'all kids doing?" she
asked.

"NOTHING!" we yelled at the same
time.

"Un… huh. Y'all better not be in
that closet trying to peek. Especially
not you," she said pointing to me. "Go
somewhere and sit down with your nappy
head."

She was always mean to Dennis and
me. Her and my mom never got along and
I guess we had to pay for that. My mom
was the oldest and she was the youngest
of eight. Perhaps my mom use to boss
her around. I know that my mom
practically raised them, especially
when their mother died of a massive
heart attack and stroke. She was very
overweight, which must have run in the
family because Auntie Bib was
overweight and so was I. On Christmas
Eve we could hardly sleep. Leslie and
I would just grab each other and scream
silently. We were so excited. Unlike
Auntie Bib, Leslie and I were crazy
about each other. All of us kids got
along very well. Besides the normal
kid stuff we were really cool.

Finally it was Christmas morning.
Auntie Bib came and woke us up.

"Come on y'all, it's time to open
up the gifts."

Grandpa wasn't there yet. He
worked at nights as a security guard at
some office building.

"Move it fat and nappy!" she
scolded at me.

"Huh name is Denise, not fat and
nappy," Dennis said. He was always
outspoken, my complete opposite.

Slap. She hit him upside his
head.

"Ain't nobody said nothing to you
with your old ugly tail. Gone

downstairs, before I beat both of y'all
tails!" she yelled.

We were both crying by this time.
We held hands to comfort each other.
Dennis and I would never have touched
anything under that tree. Especially
without Grandpa being there. He kept
Auntie Bib in check. She passed out
all of the gifts. Leslie had so many
gifts. I had two boxes. As I opened
my first one I couldn't wait. It was
clothes. I opened my other box and it
was underwear. "Where's *my* baby doll?"
I said tearfully.

"You ain't got no baby doll. You
be glad for what you got. Your
granddaddy works hard to feed y'all.
Straighten up your face. And y'all
better not touch my kids' stuff. I
can't help if y'all ain't got no mom or
daddy to buy y'all no toys."

It felt like someone had kicked me
in my heart. What really got me was
when Dennis opened our gift from
Grandpa -- it was a ball. Out of all
of those toys the only toy we got were
a ball to share. I was devastated.
Leslie and I made eye contact and she
dropped her head. It wasn't her fault.
I ran to my room. Auntie Bib ran
behind me.

"What is wrong with you? Quit
that crying before I give you something
to cry about!"

I couldn't stop crying. The more
I tried to stop, the worse I got. She
got her belt and started whipping me.

As I hollered out in pain all the kids ran in the room. Guess who else got a beating? Dennis. All of her kids were in the room but she beat Dennis. Dennis lay in Leslie's bed across from mine.

"Why us no got no mom and daddy like ere' bonie else?" He cried.

"I don't know? We got grandpa," I said.

It was hard for us as children to verbalize what we felt, but we definitely had feelings. Later that day we did get some toys from our other family members. Vivian was the only one that didn't treat us with love. Later that night when we had gone to bed Leslie came over to my bed.

"Here, Denise." She handed me the baby doll that I wanted. "Don't tell my mom. I love you," she said, giving me a kiss.

"I love you, too. Thank you."

I will never forget that Christmas. School kids were mean to me too. I guess when you are fat you aren't supposed to eat. I remember one time in seventh grade I was in the cafeteria and all I had was the same lunch as all the other students, but that day it peeved one of the cheerleaders.

"Look at Miss Fatty. Are you hungry? I bet you're always hungry. Did they give it enough to fill its belly?" she asked throwing a French fry at me.

I just held my head down. My cousin wasn't with me that day and I had no friends but hers. The other girls with her laughed. One of the girls joined in.

"Hey. I want to feed it too," she said.

They threw their fries at me and laughed as they went to their table. I just got up, with tears in my eyes and threw my food away. By the time they were done my appetite was gone.

"Yikes! Here she comes," one of the girls said as I passed by. They all screamed in horror.

One of them shouted, "It's one thing to be fat, but to be fat and ugly, that is messed up. God had to be sleeping threw that creation."

They all laughed. Kids can really be cruel. I wasn't accepted at school and especially not at home.

As the years went on, Vivian's kids were the only ones to have birthday parties and they got new clothes every school year. They had it all. Although Granddaddy loved us, he didn't think about stuff like that. Those are responsibilities that mothers handled. Leslie was so good to me, but the older we got the more I resented her. I hated the fact that she had a mother. I hated the fact that although her parents weren't together, she still had a relationship with her dad. I was taller than the average kid my age and I was fat. Leslie, on the other hand,

was beautiful. Aunt Bib made sure that
the world knew how beautiful her baby
was. Auntie Bib's kids pictures always
ended up on the mantle piece. Dennis
and I ended up being a bookmark in the
bible or a coaster for the company's
drink.

When I turned 16, my granddaddy
died. He wasn't sick it, was just his
time to go. At the reading of his will
he left his house to me. I couldn't
obtain the deed until I was 21, but it
was mine -- all paid for. It would've
gone to my mom, but he actually thought
of me. Bib and her family moved out. We
stayed in the house. Our relatives
checked on us regularly, however, we
were very mature for our age. This was
fine with both Dennis and me. Damond
and Leslie had already graduated from
high school. Leslie was going to
school to be a nurse. Damond worked at
the mall as a manager in one of the
clothing stores. Leon and Dennis were
both in the 10th grade. I was a junior
in high school and I hated everyday of
it. Once Leslie left, all my
popularity went out of the door. I was
never Denise, I was known as Leslie's
fat cousin. She had all the guys. No
one ever paid any attention to me. The
thing is, I have seen fat girls with
boyfriends -- what was it about me?
Now, Dennis was a whole different
story. Girls were constantly on the
phone or over the house. He was a
'Romeo'. I didn't even have female

friends.   I would talk to people in class, but outside of school it was just me and my brother whenever he was home.   I graduated from high school in the top ten percent of my class.   I wanted to go to college but I had no stamina and no one to give me the encouragement that I needed.   I would often slip into depression because I felt worthless.   All of my life I was talked down to by the "mother figure" in my house.   My other family members had their own affairs to tend to.   The only thing that Dennis and I shared was the hatred that we had for my aunt. Her hatefulness was his drive but it was my fall.   I had no mother, and the only father I knew was dead.   Leslie was the closest thing I had to a best friend, but being around her only reminded me of how inadequate I was. After I graduated I got a job at one of the local grocery stores as a cashier. I was eventually moved up to head cashier and then manager.   The highlight of my days would be coming home and tending to my house until one day I met this man who would change life as I knew it.

"Ma'am. Hi. I was wondering if I could write a check for more than the amount of purchase so that I can get some money back?" he asked.

"Well, sir, that depends on a lot of things. Can I see your check?" I asked.

"You sure can. Here's my identification too." He said handing me his driver's license.

"First of all, sir, this is a church check and secondly, the bank is out of town. I need to know how much over you want to write the check out for."

"Well, I am the pastor of this church and we were about to go out of town for service. I was going to buy refreshments for the members and have some money for offering without going back to the church for another check."

"If that is the case then I will put my initials on the check now." Although I didn't go to church often, I knew to have the utmost respect for the people of the cloth.

"Thank you, Ma'am," he smiled while pushing his shopping cart up the aisle. When he was done he came by the office to say thanks again.

"I want to invite you to one of our services. The church is right up the street a few miles. Do you go to church anywhere?"

"I have to be honest. I haven't been to church in about six months. When was Easter?"

"That was about six months ago. That's o.k. You can start this Sunday."

"I'll think about it." I wasn't used to people being this kind to me.

It was something different about his
smile.

"Good. I'll look forward to
seeing you and that pretty smile on
Sunday."

Did he say pretty? That's a first
especially since he wasn't talking
about my clothes. He said I had a
pretty smile. Heck, if for no other
reason I decided go to church for that.
I went to the service and it was nice.
I couldn't get into the sermon for
watching him. He was not the most
handsome man but he was a charmer.

"So, how'd you enjoy the service?"
He asked.

"It was nice."

"We always have dinner after
service. Would you like to stay and
join us?"

"No. I'll just go on home. I'm
not much for crowds."

"Come on. You'll be fine. For
me?"

As much as I hated to hang around,
something in his voice convinced me
that I was welcome.

"I will stay but I won't stay
long."

They had a spread, too. Ham,
roast, dressing, macaroni and cheese,
collard greens, yams, fried corn, fried
chicken, string beans, corn bread,
potato salad, peach cobbler, chocolate
cake, and sweet potato pie. If you name
it I am sure they had it. I mean those
women could cook. They served him hand

and foot. He made sure that I had all I wanted and he wouldn't even let me help. I found out that the Reverend was a widow. His wife had died about six years ago. They had no children. He was about 30 or maybe a little older. No wonder those women were gawking at me like that. I didn't come for him and I knew he didn't want me, yuck. As I got ready to leave he jumped up to walk me to my car. He made sure that I had a plate to go. I had never felt so warmed -- not by a man anyway.

"Was everything good to you?" He asked.

"Everything was delightful." I was not used to all of this attention. It felt funny, but I could get used to it. I continued to come to the church and he continued to make me welcome. One day he blew my mind and asked me out to dinner -- not with the church, but just the two of us. I went and it was really enjoyable. He asked me about being saved. I told him I thought that I was, I mean, I was always a good person. I would do anything for anybody - even Auntie Bib. If she needed, me I would help her. He told me that I needed to be saved and be baptized in order to go to heaven. He was a preacher, and they were closer to God than any other people so I decided to do it. This man made me feel like I was somebody. Reverend Tommy Mitchell was his name. If he

were my age I would pray for him to be
my husband. I did have feelings for
him, but of course he was just being
nice. I repeated the sinner's prayer
and got baptized on that next Sunday.
Things were really looking differently
in my eyes. I was still fat, but if it
didn't matter to God why did it matter
to anyone else? Rev. Mitchell didn't
seem to notice. He made me feel as if
I was a queen. He continued to take
me to dinner and we became good
friends. Dennis was not too fond of me
dating, but if I was happy so was he.
Leslie was thrilled that I was even
going out publicly, and it wasn't
pertaining to work.

Leslie was engaged to be married
in a year or so. I always knew that
she would get married. I never thought
that I would. Who would want me? One
Sunday after service Rev. Mitchell
asked me to come in his office.

"Have a seat Sister Denise."

"What's the problem?"

"We're going to have to stop going
out to dinner the way we've been going.
My deacons says that it doesn't look
good, you know."

"Yes, I understand." My heart was
in my throat. It was all I could do to
not cry. "That's fine," I said.

"I decided to rectify this
situation today. I want to know if you
will marry me?"

"What?"

"Yes, that's right I want you to be my wife. Will you?"

"I don't know. I want to, but I've never -- I mean..."

"Just say yes."

"Yes." I was shocked. Here I am 19 years old and I am marrying an older man that's a minister. I have never so much as kissed a boy other than someone in my family. "Why me? There are so many other women in your church that I am sure would die for this opportunity. And they look better..."

He interrupted. "Ah... ah... ah... don't even say it. Beauty is inside, not outside. You have a treasure that no one has tapped into and I am not going to pass it up."

He grabbed me and kissed me and I was sold.

"Now, I don't believe in long engagements. So what do you think about us setting the date two months from today?"

"Yes." I was thrilled to death. My whole family was glad with the exception of Auntie Bib. She was so angry with me. Leslie gave me a bridal shower, and it was beautiful. Auntie Bib's problem was not the fact that I was getting married to a minister, but the fact that anyone wanted to marry me. I refused to let her destroy my marital bliss. Although Leslie knew her mom was wrong she found a way to justify her cruelty to Dennis and me. Auntie Bib and Dennis fought

constantly. I would just ignore her,
but he would curse her out. One day
they actually fought, and she had a
restraining order put on him. He
stopped going to her home. I had to
have my things moved over to Reverend
Mitchell's house the Thursday before
the wedding. His house was like a
mansion with a housekeeper and all. He
said all he wanted from me was for me
to be his wife.

Dennis would stay at the house,
but not alone of course. My only
concern was that he kept it up,
however, since Rev.'s house was in
good hands I decided to make a point of
going by there once a week. We had a
private ceremony at the chapel behind
the church with just our closest
friends and family in attendance. His
mom was blind but as sweet as sugar.
She lived with him.

His dad had died in the wreck with
his wife. The church was on a trip and
their bus collided with a tractor-
trailer. The bus flipped over several
times and landed in a ditch. Out of 30
people that were on the bus, four died.
The rest were injured but they got
better.

The reception was huge with at
least 250 people in attendance. There
were so many gifts and cards that I got
a few ugly looks from some of the
sisters, but nothing could ruin my day,
so I thought. Auntie Bib had too much
to drink prior to the reception and it

was more than my brother wanted to deal
with.

"I ain't never seen no ugly bride,
but I guess it's a first time for
everything," Auntie Bib said.

"Mother please, not here, not
today. People will hear you," Leslie
said trying to quiet her down.

"I don't care. He must be as
drunk as I am to want to marry her.
Look at her. Looking like a big old
barracuda. Aha... ha..."

"Can't you have a little respect?"
Dennis asked.

"Oh shut up. What do you know
about respect? You are too close to me
anyway. I have a restraining order on
you. Move big headed..."

"LOOK! I will not let you mess up
my sister's happy day. You need to
step outside and collect yourself or
leave!"

"I ain't got to go no where. I'm
the mom you both never had. You leave
fool."

"Come on mother let's go out
side," Leslie said. Damond and Dennis
tried to lift her up.

"Get your hands off of me!"

By this time all eyes were on her.
Despite her threats they continued to
try to help her outside. I was so
embarrassed. The next thing I heard
was this big slap. She slapped Dennis.
What did she do that for? He ran
outside and I ran behind him.

"Dennis! Please come back," I said following him to his car.

"I am sick of her." Instead of going to the driver's side of the car he went to the passenger's side.

"Dennis, what are you doing?"

"What does it look like?" He reached into his glove compartment and pulled out a gun.

"No! Put it back!" I yelled.

"I should've done this a long time ago. She took away my life. She messed us up as kids. I hate that witch!"

"Please, this is my wedding!"

"And that's why I have to do this."

Leslie and Demond had just stepped outside with her. Everything happened so fast. Before I could scream he had gone up to Auntie Bib and BOOM! BOOM! BOOM! Three shots. I fainted. When I came back to myself people were all yelling and screaming. Dennis was gone. The paramedics arrived shortly after but it was too late. Auntie Bib was dead. Leslie and her brothers wept sorely. I couldn't believe it. How could Dennis end up like my daddy? We had no contact with him. I mean, I hated her just as much as he did, but I never could've imagined cold-blooded murder. The thing that blew my mind is he shot her exactly where my dad shot my mother. She was shot in the head, in the chest, and outside of a church. Yep, my dad shot my mom outside of church one Sunday morning. She was a

Christian, but he wasn't. He wanted
her to come home with him and she
refused. So he waited outside. They
argued, and he shot her. It was on the
news and everything.

We had Auntie Bib's funeral within
a week at our church. I felt like it
was my fault. Just like I couldn't
blame Leslie for her mom's actions I
cannot except responsibility for what
my brother did. At the funeral Leslie
was apologizing for what her mom had
done to us and I was apologizing for
Dennis. Although he was dead wrong for
what he did our family didn't stop
loving him. Dennis' trial was short
and to the point. He pleaded guilty
and he got life in the prison for
manslaughter.

Rev. Mitchell and I didn't get to
go on our honeymoon until that
following summer. I ended up renting
the house out to one of members of the
church, which was fine with me. We
started off our marriage with a literal
bang. After a few months I started to
feel the envy from the women in the
church. They just didn't like me. It
wasn't all of them just this particular
group that hung together almost like a
gang. I would walk in sometimes and
find that all conversation would stop.
I hated that. It didn't bother me
until the honey started leaking out of
my moon. With my husband being the
Pastor long hours were required at the
church doing revivals, seminars, etc.

When he would get home sometimes he
would fall asleep in his clothes. I
hadn't bargained for this. It beat
being alone. Even though I found
myself lonely with a husband. Go
figure. I wanted the ladies at the
church to like me. Maybe if I lost
some weight I would fit in. I was 5'8"
and 250+ pounds. I did just that. It
took about a year, but I had actually
lost 125 pounds. I felt so good about
myself. It didn't even matter that
those women didn't like me. As far as
I was concerned I didn't care to be
their friend anyway. My husband who
previously said that beauty was on the
inside couldn't keep his hands off of
me. That was a far cry from how we
started off but I wasn't complaining.
We couldn't go anywhere without men
turning their heads at me. This was
cool. I wasn't ever going to cheat on
my husband, but the attention was
flattering. He hated it.

"What are you smiling about?"
"I thought that was what initially
attracted you to me."
"I don't like men staring at you."
"I can't help that Tommy."
"Well, you sure don't discourage
it."
"Are you jealous?"
"Frankly, yes. I would appreciate
it if you would at least respect me and
not smile and flirt in my face."

"O.k. honey, I'm sorry." I reached to hug him, and he pushed me away. I know he wasn't tripping on me. Women were constantly making advances at him. They acted like he was a pop star instead of a minister. Just because I didn't say anything didn't mean I didn't notice. I figured that if I was faithful surely he was. If anyone had grounds to worry it would be me. He is at the church more than he is at home. Women flock at his beck and call. Those same women that hate me love him. Now that was a twist of fate. Tension built between us. I sunk into depression again and began to gain weight -- everyone noticed.

"Are you expecting?" asked one of the ladies that disliked me.

"No. Why do you ask?"

"It just looked as if you were putting on a little weight that's all."

"That is all that I am doing, putting on weight."

"Well you must be either real happy or real miserable. Which one is it?"

"Why do you even care? You don't even speak to me." I shocked myself.

"Well, if you would make yourself more approachable maybe I would speak."

It was as if she was waiting for an opportunity to say this to me. It seemed almost rehearsed.

"Well, let's start with a clean slate. My name is Sister Denise Mitchell, and you are?"

"I am Sister Nancy Jones. I am
pleased to meet you."

"The pleasure is all mine."

I couldn't believe it. Maybe I
was finally fitting in. She and I
began to talk from time to time between
services. One day I invited her over
to the house for lunch. We talked for
hours. Nancy was really down to earth.
I wondered why she hung with those
women that always kept something going?
Maybe she was like me and needed to fit
in. She acted totally different out of
their presence. She was married with
four children. Her youngest child was
my age. She was more like a mother to
me helping me with some of my marital
issues and everything. I finally told
her about my mother and what I
experienced as a child. She said that
she would be my Godmother. Those women
couldn't stand it. She actually began
to wean herself from them and we began
to bond more. By the time I had been
married five years I was 24. I was
ready to have kids. Tommy had me on
the pill all of this time and I felt
that we should discuss having at least
two children. I was tired of just
being his wife. He was hardly ever
home and my biological clock was
ticking. I decided to discuss it with
him over dinner that night. Sister
Nancy said the way to a man's heart was
through his stomach. I made chicken
Alfredo, steamed vegetables, tossed
salad, and hot homemade rolls and

butter. I had the cinnamon candles lit all over the place with rose petals leading to the dining room. I put on my silk lavender teddy with the sheer jacket and fur slippers to match. I put on his favorite cologne "French Vanilla Musk". That fragrance always got me compliments. It had a sweet smell that almost seemed to make you float. I topped it off with the surround sound system playing some soft slow jazz music.

"What's all this for?"

"Baby, I want to talk to you about something. We have been married for a while now, and I am ready to have some children. I will be twenty five soon and I am ready to make you a daddy."

"I am not ready for any more kids."

"Anymore kids. What do you mean? You said your wife didn't have any kids. What anymore?"

"Look, I don't feel like talking about this. I'll be back."

He got up from the table, and walked out of the house. A few minutes later I heard the car pull off. It felt as though he stabbed me with a dagger in my heart. I sat there and cried for about an hour and then I called Sister Nancy. She thought I knew and she refused to tell me what I missed. One thing was definitely sure, Tommy wasn't that sweet man that I first met. Maybe I did marry him too

soon. He is definitely a Dr. Jeckle
and Mr. Hyde. Sometimes I wake up and
find him staring at me. It was as if
his eyes were glowing in the dark.

One day I was watching a
television evangelist and he said, "If
you want to know something and you
can't find the answers, fall on your
knees and talk to Jesus. He keeps no
secrets."

So I did just that. I did this
three nights in a row. The third night
I felt this thick presence in the room
with me. As I began to pray this voice
interrupted me. It made me feel so
comfortable. It said, "Don't worry
about anything. I am a prayer answering
God and I am with you. Rest in me and
I will reveal mysteries unto you. Fret
no longer, I will answer thee in three
days. Look for me to answer."

I jumped up with this assurance
that everything was going to be all
right. I begin to praise God because I
knew that He had visited me. I was
stretching my hands and hollering,
"Yes, Lord!" When I came to myself, I
looked around and Tommy was staring at
me with this cold piercing glaze in his
eyes. I was with God and I wasn't
scared of him anymore. The next night
that evangelist was on again. He had
my full attention. He was teaching
about a heavenly language and touching
these people who were falling out like
flies. I started feeling that presence
again. Then the speaker said, "If you

want the fire in your life at home
touch the screen in faith and receive
the Holy Ghost."

Tommy never talked about the Holy
Ghost as if it were a gift, just as if
it were a feeling. I found out that
night that it was more than a feeling.
As I touched that screen I begin to
speak in tongues as the Spirit gave me
utterance. It felt so good,
indescribably good. If I had wings I
could've taken flight. The next night
I went to pray and it happened again. I
was speaking in another tongue and it
was phenomenal. It was as if I had
been walking on the desert for hours
and found a lemonade stand with the
coldest, sweetest drink there was. I
did get an answer but not a verbal one.
This third day fell on a Sunday and I
didn't know what to expect. I didn't
ride with Tommy this morning, but came
early to pray. When I got to the
church Sister Terri was in the parking
lot sitting in her car. This was
strange because no one is early except
the Deacons or the janitorial staff. I
walked over to her car just to make
sure that she was fine. She was one of
the women that didn't care much for me.

"Good morning, Sister Terri. How
are you?"

"I am fine, and you?" She was
looking me up and down as if I was
trash to be taken out.

"Why are you just sitting out
here?"

"I was supposed to meet somebody," she said short and abruptly.

"O. K. I'll be inside."

She didn't have to tell me that her being there was none of my business. I didn't have to know. Sister Terri is married to the head of the Deacon's board. They have two of the cutest boys, who are almost teens, maybe around 11 and 12. Perhaps they were tall for their ages. I prayed for about twenty minutes when I heard the Lord say, "Watch as well as pray."

I didn't get it. He said it two more times. I got up from the altar and walked slowly over to the window and who did I see? It was Tommy and Terri talking and walking to his office. What was the big secret? People always meet with Tommy. What did she have to hide? Was she sleeping with my husband? She had to have more scruples than that. If I was going to cheat surely it wouldn't be anyone that I knew this closely. When she came out of the study, service had already started. She was looking at me like she wanted to bite me and I was looking right back at her to let her know that I had teeth too. I wanted her to know that she no longer intimidated me. I noticed something that was really strange. Sister Terri's second son was coughing uncontrollably during the sermon. As I looked at him when he sat up I almost fainted. It was as if Tommy sat up. Surely this was not his

child. How could I have missed
something so obvious? That little boy
looked as if Tommy spit him out. Oh
God. What have I gotten myself into?
That is why she hates me. It has
nothing to do with my looks but
everything to do with my husband. Is
this what Sister Nancy wouldn't tell
me? I heard the Lord say, "Brace
yourself, there is more to come. Be
quick to hear and slow to speak".

After church I ran to Sister Nancy
and told her we had to talk.

"What is it?" She asked coldly.

"Did Tommy have a baby with Sister
Terri?"

"Who told you that?" She pulled
me to the side.

"No one told me anything. Is it
true?"

"I shouldn't get involved. Ask
your husband." She left me standing
there. I couldn't believe this was
happening. I couldn't cry, but I sure
wanted to. I didn't go to Tommy at
that time. It wasn't until the next
piece of the puzzle came to me. Here I
am, first lady and there is so much
that I am not aware of about my
husband, but God won't keep you in the
dark. If you seek, you shall find. I
was very observant during the next
Sunday service. As the choir was
singing I just happened to look in the
band at the drummer. I always thought
that he was cute, but this time he
looked kind of funny. I looked at

Tommy then back at Andre. No. Come
on. This boy looks just like Tommy
too. His mom was over the nurse's
committee. How many women has Tommy
been with? He's the preacher. Maybe
all of this was in my head. I had to
leave out. It was out of order to walk
during the service, but I felt faint
and weak. As I staggered towards the
door I noticed the usher looked like a
female version of Tommy. I got out of
there like there was a fire chasing me.
All of those women that gawked at me
when I first got there *knew* Tommy in
every sense of the word. What type of
mess was I apart of? Were we all his
wives? Was Sister Nancy one too?
When Tommy got home I asked him, and he
didn't deny it. I asked him why he
hadn't told me. He said men have needs
and that God understood. The problem
wasn't with God it was with me. He was
taking advantage of his authority with
all of these women. I wasn't going to
be a part of it. He said that he would
never divorce me and that was fine. I
didn't think that I could trust another
man enough to marry again. I informed
the family that was living in my house
that I would not be renewing their
lease and that they would need to have
another place of residency by the time
the lease was up. I stayed with Tommy
until the lease was up. We were no
longer living as man and wife, but more
like roommates. He made a few sexual
advances towards me but I could no

longer get pleasure out of an act that he had perverted.

"So. Do you have any feelings for those women at church?"

"I love my flock. Things happen. Even Paul had a thorn in his flesh and God never removed it. He was the top of the apostles and he wrote the majority of the New Testament. I know that God is with me. I have human feelings."

"But I am your wife. What about your feelings for me? What about your loyalty to me?"

"I never said that I was in love with you and neither did I lie and say that I had no other women. I've been honest with you."

"Tommy you knew what type of a woman I was when you met me. You knew that I wasn't with sharing you and had I known that you had all of these children by these women I never would've married you."

"Well, the Bible tells us to help the needy. You were as needy as they come. I knew you had never been with a man and, had I not approached you, you'd still be alone."

"How dare you disrespect me like this. You should've left me alone. No. Better yet I say thank you. If it weren't for you I wouldn't be this close to the Lord. It was God that showed me who you are. He's the One that told me all about your children. No human told me anything. His Spirit leads and guides me. That's how I can sleep at night and not fear you any more. His Word and his angels protect me."

"Woman you sound crazy. God doesn't speak to you unless you are his spokesperson, which you are not."

"What are you? You have to do more than preach it. You've got to live it."

"Ain't no sense in talking to you. You've been brainwashed by somebody, but it wasn't me."

Our conversations went on like that for the duration of my stay there. I knew that God was real and there was no way that Tommy could persuade me that the way he was living was right. Adultery had been a sin since the beginning of time. I just had to pray for him. God had not made anyone that He can't handle. I just prayed that Tommy saw the light before it was too late.

I found the church that the evangelist was the pastor of. It was almost two hours away but it was worth the drive. I visited for a few months and then joined. I am on their intercessory prayer team and am seeking my divorce from Tommy. Adultery was major grounds for divorce. I wanted no parts of the masquerade. As long as I was hooked up with him I was hooked up to a curse. I prayed for him that one day God would truly save him and show him his wrong. I maintained my weight

and am now a size 12 and plan to stay
that way. I found out that I didn't
need man's acceptance, only God's. I
became happy with who I was and loved
me and that's all that mattered.

My prayer team was able to hook up
a service at the prison where Dennis is
in. Guess what? He eventually got
saved. The most ironic thing was our
father was in the same prison. I still
harbor resentment and pray daily that
God would cleanse me of this. I talked
to my dad from time to time. God
helped one day at a time. I decided
that I would continue to serve Him and
with much prayer and fasting I would be
delivered.

I couldn't believe how much I
looked like my dad. The more I talked
to him, the more I felt his remorse.
The more remorseful he was the more
sympathetic I became. No matter how
hard he tried there was no way that he
could change what happened in either
one of our pasts. We just had to move
on. If God could forgive him, so
could I. I looked forward to the day
when we could all fellowship together.
If not here, I knew we'd meet in
heaven.

Chapter Three

PAULA

As a child, I went from foster home to foster home. My mother gave me up for adoption at birth. She was 14 and didn't want to have an abortion so to her this was the only option. The family that was initially supposed to adopt me got caught doing illegal things with some of the other kids they had adopted and the department of family and children's services quickly removed me. Ever since then I went from pillar to post. The older you were, the less likely you were to find a permanent home. I also had the issue of being mixed. I hated that word because it's not as though I were some type of food or combination of food. Mixed was better than being called half-breed. My mom was white and my dad was black. I would have preferred the phrase "mixed up". That described me perfectly. White and black people had issues with me. I was too dark and my hair was too curly to be considered white. On the other hand I was too light skinned and my hair was too "good" to be considered black. I remember once I was with one of my foster families. The Jones' lived in a suburb in Cleveland, Ohio called

Bedford Heights. This area was predominantly white, but my foster parents were black. I was about 6 years old. We had gone to the grocery store and I was walking down the candy aisle. Mrs. Jones said that I could go over there to get candy to buy. There was an older white lady behind me.

"Hey little girl. What are you up to?"

"My mother said that I could pick up some candy to buy. It's so many I don't know which one to get."

"You are the prettiest little thing. Do you want me to help you?"

"No thanks. I am not supposed to talk to strangers." The lady followed me over to the next aisle and when she saw Mrs. Jones she looked as if she had seen a ghost. She began to choke.

"Is this your, grandchild?" she asked Mrs. Jones.

"No. She is my daughter. My foster daughter."

"Oh, I thought as much. She looks nothing like you. Why are you trying to adopt a white child?"
I am thinking who's white?

"If it's any of your concern she is black."

"She doesn't look like she belongs with your kind that's all."

"How dare you say such a thing especially in front of this child? You ought to be ashamed of yourself."

"The shame is you. You should've gotten your own kind is all I am

saying. You people are so sensitive."
She walked away.

"Mrs. Jones why doesn't she want
you to have me?" I asked.

"Paula, some people in this world
are so ignorant. I am sorry that you
had to hear that."

"That lady didn't like you, did
she?"

"Well, some people think that we
are not as good as they are because of
the color of our skin. God doesn't see
no difference."

"What color am I?"

"You are black like me."

"No I am not. I am white."

"No sweetie, your mom was white,
but your daddy was black and the makes
you black."

"So why does my arm look white
when yours is brown?"

"We are people of color and just
because your skin color is light you
are still black."

"So why is my skin her color and
not yours?"

"It is hard to explain. You'll
understand it when you get older."

The next couple of years I lived
with them then I was taken away and
placed with a white family. They lived
in Akron, Ohio. I hated their house.
Not because they were white, but
because they hated blacks. I couldn't
understand. Mrs. Jones said we are all
special to God no matter how different
we are. Well the Davis' thought that

because my mom was white, I was white and they wanted to instill "the right values" in me. They said that I couldn't help that my nigger daddy took their prize.

By the time I left there I was confused. I didn't know what to think. I knew that I had to get out so I tried to be as bad as I could. They weren't allowed to hit me, and though the Jones' hit me, I felt love. The Davis' didn't hit me, and I felt horrible. Was I black or white? Why did it matter? One thing everyone thought is that I was a beautiful kid. I began doing outlandish things like stealing from the grocery store, the mall, or where ever we went. I always played with matches. Once I set the kitchen on fire. I was a hellion. I stole so much, but I would never get caught. All I was doing was accumulating goods. It got to the point that I quit doing it to get in trouble and continued because I liked it. No one ever suspected me. Even with security guards and mirrors and cameras I some how avoided getting caught. I actually got bold enough to take things off of people. By the time I was 14 I was stealing for friends. I had finally got some stability in my life. Tyrone and Alicia Thompson adopted me. They had one child of their own. Her name was Tylicia. She and I were the same age. They lived in East Cleveland. I attended Shaw High School where I wasn't treated any differently than anyone else. Most of the kids knew Licia.

We both were very popular. I just had this major fetish with stealing. I would steal anything from pencils to clothes. One day I almost got caught. We were at Severance Mall and Licia saw this jacket she wanted, and our mom said it was too expensive. Licia knew that I would steal little stuff, but she had no idea of how deep I was in. Not until that day did when we almost got busted.

"Licia, go in the dressing room and act like you are trying on these clothes. I'll put the jacket underneath my coat when you call the saleslady in the dressing room for help. She doesn't know that we are together any way."

"Girl, we can't do that. We will get caught for sure.
How will we explain this to mom?"

"See, first of all you look suspicious. All you are doing is asking for help. Don't worry about mom. Once we get out of the store, I'll keep it under my coat and we'll keep it in one of our lockers at school. We'll think of something else later."

"No girl, I can't get in trouble."

"Just watch. I am going to leave the store when she goes in the back. The other lady isn't even watching. Come on."

"O.K. If you get caught I am not in it."

"Cool."

We went on as planned. Everything went smoothly until I got to the door. There was a security guard at the door. How did I miss that?

"Umm... excuse me young lady. Do you mind stepping over here?" he asked.

"What's the problem?"

"I saw you over by the jewelry and now you're leaving so quickly with no bags. Let me check your pockets."

I let him. He was so stupid. He didn't even notice that I had two big heavy coats on. He actually checked the pockets of their jacket.

"Sorry about that young lady. Just doing my job."

"That's o.k. When you are innocent you have no reason to run. Have a nice day officer, sir."

Licia couldn't believe that we got away with it. A few weeks after that, Mom surprised Licia with the jacket. We took that one back and got the money for it. Licia simply started wearing the one that I got. No one was ever the wiser.

By the time I was a senior in high school I was into boys so the petty theft thing was a bit played. I still had sticky fingers from time to time, but I was into a new career -- MEN. I liked older guys and they loved me. It wasn't a sex thing because I was not interested in that. I was actually

scared of it. Mom always told Licia
and me that we had plenty of time for
that. I did have a few guys that tried
to make sexual advances, but I'd set
them straight. If they got mad it was
on to the next guy. I was strong-
willed and there was no pressuring
being done except by me. Both my
sister and I vowed to keep our
virginity until we were married or at
least on our own. We learned from what
happened to me that we didn't want to
bring any children in the world and
have to give them up or have to
struggle with being able to take care
of them. Once I was a senior in high
school, I was dealing with grown men.
They were smoother than the boys in
school were. I needed a man with a car
because I was always going somewhere.

The last guy that I was seeing was
trouble. My parents didn't want me
seeing him because he was too old. He
was 23 and so fine and sported a neat
low haircut, had greenish brown eyes
and the prettiest smile with a small
gap between the top two front teeth.
He was rather short about 5' 8" and was
so bow legged that you would swear he
was a cowboy. I ended up sneaking
around and making up lies to be with
him. He thought that I was 18, and I
didn't say otherwise. Once I graduated
we came out of the closet. Then he
tried to make me do that sex thing, and
I wasn't having it. We broke up and I

moved on. It did hurt a little because
I really liked this guy. Oh well.

That fall Licia went to Bowling
Green University and I went to Central
State -- we both cried like babies.
Since I have been with them we have
never been apart. We had our sisterly
spats, but that was my girl. I was
really going to miss my parents too.
They were so good to us.

My major was accounting, and I was
determined to always have fat pockets
and to keep my own books. I knew how
roguish I was so I wasn't about to
trust anyone else with my money.
College was a whole different world
than high school. There were no little
boys -- these were men. A sea of
opportunity and I was just the one with
the bait and the fishing rod. I was
very particular about my men. He
needed a car, a decent job or steady
cash flow and had to be a sharp dresser
especially if they weren't that cute.
During my freshman year, I met a bunch
of losers. If I wasn't giving up the
goods neither were they. By my senior
year, I landed a real prospect. He was
a professor, which was against the
rules, but he couldn't resist me. His
name was Dr. Vincent Kelley. He was
married though. I knew it was wrong
but he had all I needed; money, a Benz,
looks, and he got sex from his wife. I
had no morals about a lot of things,
but I was dead serious about sex. I
didn't want any children and HIV was a

new epidemic that I wanted no parts of. He and I dated for a few months. We did a lot of kissing and heavy petting. He got tired of my excuses quickly and, after a while, got stingy and didn't want to give me any more money. Oh well, who wants a married man anyway?

My next prospect was a white man. I had enough of brothers and they were too demanding. Since I was mixed I thought that it just might work. I met Todd at my graduation party. He wasn't actually at the party but he was in the hotel at another event. We exchanged numbers and it was on. He fit all of my qualifications. He was about four years my elder, but age was nothing but a number to me. He was sexy as they came. He looked like he should play on a soap opera. He had blonde wavy hair that he wore in one ponytail. His eyes were as blue as the summer skies on the clearest of days. He was about six feet tall and his body was that of a god. I am talking about biceps and triceps. My parents liked him and so did the rest of my family, though he was a bit uncomfortable being around blacks. He never said it, but I could feel it. He was always around white people so I don't think that he was prejudice. He was simply uninformed and definitely uncomfortable. I was crazy about him. He had his own house and everything. He took me to meet his family and this reminded me of the Davis'. His mom didn't care for me at

all.   "So, Paula what is it that
you do?" She asked.

"Well, Mrs. Lovelady. I am a C. P.
A. for a very prestigious law firm."

"Mmm... What school did you got to?"

"I graduated *Suma cum Laude,* from
Central State University." Why was I
letting this woman intimidate me? I
didn't owe her any explanations about
anything that I was doing or had done.

"How did you meet my Todd?"

"Mother we met at a social
gathering." He answered.
"I didn't ask you I want her to
answer."
"Todd answered correctly."
Dinner was long and drawn out. Besides
he and his dad talking, there was
nothing but an exchange of dirty looks
between his mother and me. I offered
to help her in the kitchen afterwards.

"I got my eye on you." She said.

"For what I said. Don't you like
black people? I asked trying to bring
out her issues.

"Black has nothing to do with it.
I know your kind. It's something there
I just can't put my finger on it. You
just rest assured that the real you
will come out."

"How dare you judge me? You don't
even know me. You haven't even given
me a chance. I will tell you this, I
am not going to let you intimidate me
and I am going to continue to see Todd.
You have a wonderful son and you should
want him to be happy."

"His happiness is my concern. Why would a black woman want a white man other than to get what he has?"

"You are really bold to ask such a question but I don't need your son's money or anything, I have my own."

"Good then."

Todd peaked into the kitchen. "Is everything alright?" He asked.

"We're fine." We both said in unison.

That was the last time that I was over there for dinner. If we went there it would only be for a quick hello. Todd proposed to me about a year after we'd been dating. I said yes and we got married six months later. To keep down confusion, we went to the justice of the peace. His mom had a major problem with it. His dad was upset, but not enough to ruin their relationship. He had an older brother that lived in Italy. I met him via telephone, but that was the extent of it. The most exciting thing was that I kept my vow to wait until I was married to give myself to anyone. I'm glad I did. It was as addictive as stealing. I would've been a nymphomaniac and a kleptomaniac if I'd had sex before. As time went on I guess Todd got bored with me. He began seeing someone else and was acting much differently than his usual "good guy" image that he portrayed while we dated. It bothered me somewhat, but I was going to get him back. Money had a way of pacifying me.

Things really started getting out of hand when the abuse began. Sometimes Todd would come home drunk, we would begin arguing, and he would beat me. As tough as I was, I couldn't believe the fear that would grip me when he hit me, and he knew that I was scared. One night I heard him come in and I knew that he had probably been drinking so I pretended to be asleep. He came in the room and threw his clothes on the bed and stood there watching me.

"I know that you aren't asleep. I saw the lights go out. Get up!"

"Todd, you are drunk and I just…" Before I could finish my sentence he hit me. He got a kick out of controlling me like that. My mind would tell me to grab the lamp or something to bang on his head, but my body would be paralyzed by the fear that I felt. He had murder in his eyes. I couldn't believe that this was the same sweet and soft-spoken man that never swore a day in his life. Now he was an abusive bully with the filthy mouth of a sailor. I wanted to leave but I needed the security that this lifestyle provided me. I never told anyone of the abuse, but it was getting out of hand. Sometimes he would even rape me. While he would be raping me, he'd call me all kinds of names. Sometimes he'd be so sexually aggressive with me that I would bleed for a couple of days like I was having

a light menstrual cycle. I didn't want
to stay, but I couldn't afford to
leave. He was making big money and so
was I, but I couldn't afford my
lifestyle without him. I was sick of
the abuse, the other women, and the
alcohol. When he started making
excuses about giving money towards our
expenses, then I knew it was time to
get paid. We had recently got our life
insurance policies revised and I was
tired of being married anyway. All
these years of hell had to pay off some
how. I could've just divorced him and
got some money, but the more he beat me
the more I wanted him dead. I was
primary beneficiary, and his policy was
worth 2.5 million dollars. I would be
set for life.

   I could never flat out murder
anyone, but if he suddenly got ill off
from some food or something, no one
would ever know. As far as anyone
knew, we had a pretty decent marriage.
I never complained about the affairs,
and he didn't know that I knew, but I
did. I actually hired a private
investigator. I had pictures and
everything. I was never in love. I
think the thought of living a
prosperous life turned me on. I was in
love with money, and he had it so I
loved him too.
I asked a friend of mine who worked as
a registered nurse at a local hospital
about getting me some drugs that would
slowly do what I needed done and not

point a finger at me. She refused at
first, but after I paid her a few
thousand in cash she came around. The
only conditions were that I was to
never mention her name. I will take it
to my grave. I begin putting it in his
meals daily. I would only give him a
small amount because I wanted him to
suffer. Death was too easy. Within
days he began to have flu-like symptoms
such as fever, vomiting, and diarrhea.
He was in the hospital the next week.
They couldn't find anything. My friend
told me that it is undetectable in
small doses and it takes a while to
accumulate. The doctors must have
gotten frustrated and just said he had
pneumonia. I knew that this wasn't the
case at all, but it made my task so
much easier. His mom knew. I don't
know how, but when she saw me she just
stared as if she could jump through me.
No one expected him to die, but I knew
the real deal. He slipped into a coma
within weeks. He was declared brain
dead. He had a written request in our
insurance papers that if anything like
that would transpire to go ahead and
pull the plug. They did just that. I
couldn't believe what I had done.
Nobody but nobody even knew. There was
no prenuptial and he left me everything
in his will. I got his house, his car,
and his money. His mom said to me at
the reading of his will.

"I know you had something to do
with it and one day I'll find out how.

My son has never been sick a day in his
life. I know what the doctors said but
that is not the truth. If you are
innocent I will apologize, but God is
going to show your true colors. You're
not even grieving. BE SURE YOUR SINS
WILL FIND YOU OUT."

Those were her last words to me.
I did feel bad, but he did me wrong and
I had to be compensated. I sold the
house and gave my parents some money.
I changed my name back to my maiden
name and moved to Manhattan, New York.
I made sure that I was unlisted because
I wanted nothing to do with anyone. I
paid my parents for taking care of me
and I wanted a fresh start. I even
started letting my new friends call me
by my middle name. Elaine Thompson was
my name. My lavish lifestyle was
almost more than my pockets could
handle. It was time to go fishing
again. I dated several men, but none
of them was what I needed. I never
dated any more black men after that guy
in college. I met this Italian man and
he was all of that. I called him
Frankie. He definitely had the look
and his bank account was swollen. I
refused to move in with him, but I
practically lived there. The thing
with him is that he wasn't trying to
marry me. He was a womanizer. I
wanted him, but I needed more money.
If I moved in I would be giving up my
freedom and my individuality. It was
either that, find another man, or stop

living large. I guess I was back on
the market.

I met a man named Harvey Sadler.
He was in his late fifties and in love
with me. He was what my sisters called
a "sugar daddy". He trusted me with
everything. I was so good to him and I
didn't mind doing anything he wanted
just as long as he kept my pockets fat.
We eventually got married. I knew that
I couldn't strike right away so I
decided to wait at least a year. One
day I had a twist of fate.

"Ring... ring..."

"Hello?" I said.

"Hi, I am calling from the Sally
Jesse Raphael Show and there is someone
that has been looking for you. It is a
surprise guest and we wanted you to be
surprised as well. If you except we
will fly you out and pay for all of
your expenses." She said.

"Is this a joke?"

"No. This is real."

"How did you get my number and who
is looking for me? You could be with
FBI or something. How do I know?"

"Trust me ma'am. It's not even
that type of show. It is family
oriented. That's about all I can tell
you without giving it away," she said.
I actually accepted. Little did I know
how much my life was about to change?
When I got on stage, Sally asked me a
series of questions. The last question
she asked before my mind was blown was
if I had any idea of who was looking

for me? My answer was no. Then the
most wonderful thing happened. My birth
mother came out. This was the lady
responsible for giving me life. I had
always thought of her, but I never
thought I could possibly find her. I
had genuine emotions. I cried and she
cried. It was beautiful. During the
interview, I didn't mention my last
husband, but I did mention that I was a
newlywed. After the show, she and I
kept in close contact. A few months
later the strangest thing happened.
Harvey was out of town. There was a
ring at the door.

"Who is it?" I asked.

"Manhattan Police department," he
said.

I opened the door with a
quickness.

"How may I help you?"

"Are you Paula Elaine Thompson-
Sadler?" He asked.

"Yes, I am."

"Ma'am you have the right to
remain silent. Anything you say will be
used against you in a court of law.
You have a right to an attorney. If
you cannot afford an attorney, one will
be appointed to you..."

"What is this about? Why are you
arresting me?" I interrupted.

"Do you understand your rights?"

"What is this for?"

"You are under arrest for the
murder of Mr. Todd Bradley Lovelady."

"Murder, he died of pneumonia."

"We'll see," he said, helping me into the back seat of the police car. Who knew? How did I get busted? Todd's mom happened to catch Sally when I was on. When I didn't mention his death, but talked totally of my new husband she found that strange. The fact that I went on as Elaine struck her as odd too. She had his body exhumed and they did an autopsy. After a forensic analysis, they found the poison in his system. They some how narrowed it down to the only two hospitals in Xenia, Ohio, that had this drug. They gave the staffs lie detectors voluntarily. The ones that refused were the ones they tested. My friend was amongst those tested. From what they threatened her with, she gave me up in a heartbeat. My own husband had to testify of his hurt of how I didn't tell him that I was a widow. I failed my lie detector test and was found guilty of murder in the first degree. I was sentenced to life in a women's penitentiary in Ohio. Once I got there, I thought that I would lose my mind.

After a year or so, I went to one of the services that they have for the women that want to attend. This evangelist was talking directly to me. She said, "Most of you all in here have had a hard life. The things that they said you did, most of you all did, but God sent his son to die for your sins.

If you accept Him, he will come in and
give hope to your hopeless situation."
All of my life, no one had given me
this chance. I thought that if they
had then maybe my destiny would be
different. I knew that I was a sinner,
but that's all. I didn't know about
heaven and hell. I thought the Bible
was a storybook. My parents hardly
ever went to church. I do remember my
foster mom, Mrs. Jones, being somewhat
religious. I felt bad -- I mean dirty.
I begin to remember all of the things
that I stole, all of the lies I've
told, the men I had cheated, and the
life that I took.   I was even planning
on doing it to Harvey. Here comes this
preacher saying that God will forgive
me through me believing His son died
for me. I don't understand. They had
us repeat this prayer for our sins and
I did. I cried like a baby. They gave
us a Bible and I begin to read. I went
to chapel every Tuesday and things
started making sense. Now that I was a
Christian, I wanted to get some things
right. I wrote letters to my parents
apologizing for embarrassing them and
practically disowning them. I wrote my
husband who has now filed for divorce
and repented to him too. I wrote to my
former mother-in-law and asked for her
forgiveness.   Whether they forgive me
or not is irrelevant. I just wanted to
get my end straight. I am going to
have to pay for what I did for the rest
of my life. I will never see freedom

on this side again. I can't say that I
deserve freedom. I am just glad that I
have forgiveness with Jesus and that no
matter what I have done he has forgiven
me and He is making me a mansion so
that I can live with him. So until I
die I will continue to cultivate my
relationship with God and witness to
the other inmates to give them hope in
the word of God. This life we have is
only temporary, but heaven will last
always. Yes, I have a debt to pay
here, but Jesus paid a debt that I
could never pay. Before I repented, He
had forgiven me and that is why I have
hope. Because he lives I can face
tomorrow, all fear is gone. Now I know
who holds my future and my life is
worth living just because Jesus lives.

Chapter Four

YVETTE

It's funny how you never expect more from life than you think it has to offer you. Well I never did. I guess what I had was what I had to live with and I thought that was good -- well as good as it was going to get. I grew up in the projects with my mom, my little sister Peaches, and my mom's current live in boyfriend, Max. She made us call him Uncle Max, but we knew what was really going on. He started staying with us when I was about nine. I hated him. Neither Peaches nor I had the same father. Peaches' daddy stayed in the next set of apartments about a mile down the street. I didn't know who my daddy was. The man mom says was my dad looks nothing like me. I was no fool I looked nothing like my mom or Peaches. Chances were mom didn't really know herself. It didn't seem to matter much to me at that time anyway.

During the summer we had so much fun in the daytime. My mom's sister Queeta stayed next door and she had five kids of her own. Everybody called them stair steps. That was the funniest thing to us. It wasn't until we got older that we realized that people were talking about the fact that

they were born so close together,
practically year after year. We would
play all day; ride our bikes; go to the
candy store; play house, jump rope,
hide and seek, kick ball; you name it,
we did it all day. Mom and Auntie
Queeta wanted us out of the house so
that they could get drunk and do
whatever it was that they did. We
would come in for lunch or maybe
something to drink, but that would be
it until the streetlights came on.
Then we had to come in bathe and get
ready for bed. This was the part I
hated. I never knew what the night
would bring for me.

It was Uncle Max. Mom would be
drunk and Peaches would be comatose
when he struck. He would come in my
room and close the door. He stunk like
beer, cigarettes, and feet. I don't
know if he ever took a shower. He'd be
breathing hard and he would be fondling
me. I was just a little kid with no
shape at all. What was he getting out
of this? I knew that he did things
like this with my mom, but why me? I
would rather it was me and not Peaches.

"What are you scared of? I ain't
gone hurt you 'less you say something.
Ain't nobody gone believe you anyway,"
he said, whispering and blowing his
cigarette breath in my face. Then he
would make me take off my panties and
he'd feel on me. I felt filthy and
grimy. Then he would make me touch it
-- his penis. He'd make me put that

big old stinking thing in my mouth. I
would be crying and gagging. It was
horribly disgusting. He'd threaten to
beat and kill me if I would ever tell.
Then he would leave. I would run to
the bathroom to wash my mouth and scrub
everything else. I felt like I was
corrupt or something. I wanted to tell
my mom, but she would kill me, I knew
it. I surely couldn't tell Auntie
Queeta because she would tell mom.
Peaches was younger than me and she
would understand even less. This went
on for years. I guess mom really liked
this uncle. He got so bold that he
started messing with me in broad
daylight. Mom would be gone and we'd
be outside. He'd call me in.

"Uh… Yvette? Can you come fix me
something to drink? he asked.

"Ok. Come on y'all," I'd say
hoping that the kids would follow. No
one did, they just kept on playing.

"You know I need you?", he asked.

"Do you want some water or some
kool aid?" He brushed his big body
parts against me.

"I want a tall drank of Yvette,"
he said rubbing and squeezing my butt.
By this time I was about 14, so I had a
shape and had also started my monthly
periods. That didn't even make any
difference to him. He would make me
watch porno movies with him while he
rubbed on his manhood. I think the
reason that I was so developed at 14

was because of his constant fondling of
me.

This one particular time he went
all of the way. He actually penetrated
my vagina. I screamed out in pain and
disgust.

"Shut up!" he yelled.

"It hurts!" I squalled. He
slapped me so hard that my ears started
ringing. I said nothing else. He
groaned and moaned. I laid there with
tears streaming down my face. When he
was done he got up. He was
apologizing, then the next thing I knew
he was threatening me again. I was
bleeding on the sheets and down my
legs. I didn't know if I was on my
cycle or not. I got in the tub to wash
that filth off of me and then I got in
my bed. I remember Peaches finally
coming in.

"Are you sick 'vette?" she asked.

"I don't know what's wrong with
me. I will be ok."
About a month or so after that I really
did get sick. I was at school and out
of no where I got this uncontrollable
urge to throw up. It happened so fast
that I couldn't make it to the
bathroom. I went to the nurse's office
and they sent me home. Mom was drunk
as usual.

"What you sick of girl?" she asked

"I don't know. I just had to throw
up."

"I know you ain't been letting no
boys feel on you? When was the last
time you had your period?"

"I don't know."

"Well, what you mean you don't
know. You been messing around with
some boys?"

"No ma'am."

"You is kind of getting fat."
Now I knew that she was drunk. I was
as little as they came. 4'11" and
about 102 pounds. There was nothing
fat about me. I was very developed,
but everyone called me little bit.

"Well, go in there and lay down.
If you get sick tomorrow we going down
to the free clinic and you better not
be pregnant!" she yelled.
I was scared. What if I was? How
could I explain this? I didn't even
like kissing boys, but there would be
no convincing mom otherwise. I was
almost sure that I was pregnant. I
didn't ask for this. What would I do?
Mom always said she wasn't about to be
a grandmother and if one of us got
pregnant that we would have to get an
abortion or get out. As fate would
have it I got sick the next day, and we
went to the clinic. I was pregnant.
Here I am 14 years old with no
boyfriend, just a perverted "uncle". I
had no choice in whether I got molested
and now I have to make a decision to
keep a life, my baby, or lose my home.
What do I do?

"Who is the daddy, Yvette?" Mom asked.

"I can't say."

"Don't be crying now. You should've been crying while your legs was opened."

"Let me talk to her Kiki," Auntie Queeta said. We went to my room and I told her everything.

"That old dog. I ought to kill him. Baby I am so sorry. Why didn't you come and tell me?" she asked crying.

"He said he'd kill me and I believed him. I don't want to have an abortion, to me that's like murder. I did good without my dad and so will my baby."

"Are you sure you want his baby?"

"Of course not. It will just be my baby. No one has to know but you, mom, and close family. I'll take being called something that I am not in order to keep my baby."

"Well, once your mom hears this she ain't gone want him in this house no more."

We told my mom and she flipped the script big time.

"Why you gone lie on him like that? He hasn't done any mess like that. You little whore you don't want to accept responsibility for what you did so you gone blame an innocent man. Why didn't you tell me before now, because you're lying? You just mad cause he ain't your daddy!"

"Mom, I promise that I am not lying. Why would I lie about this? I am only 14 and I don't even talk to boys. You have never known me to be fast. Why don't you believe me?"

"I know you lying. Ain't no man gone do that to no little girl!"

"Mom, let's ask him together. Please believe me."

"I ain't asking him nothing because I know that he didn't do it. You ain't keeping it anyway."

"Mom, I can't kill my baby."

"Ain't no baby! Shut up all that crying! You aren't fooling anybody with those crocodile tears. How you gone take her side Queeta?"

"Now Kiki, you know this child ain't gone just sit here and make this up. Kids don't even think like that. Heck, I don't know no grown ups that think like that. That is just sick. You gone choose your man over your child is what I can't believe."

"You know what? You and your lying niece can get out of my house. I will not be disrespected and lied to by neither you nor her. She ain't gone be nothing but a little whore any way. Just like us -- in the projects having babies and collecting welfare. Our mother did it, and we just passing down the torch to the next whore," she said leaving the house.

"Mom, don't say that. I'm not a whore and neither are you..."

"I don't believe you gone let your child go like this."

"Mommy, I love you. Please! I need you. Listen to me. Help me. I only have one mother and I don't know what to do!"

"You can take your little lying tail and stay with your new mother, Queeta, because I ain't got time to deal with this. When I get back I want you gone. And don't you tell your sister these lies. I don't want her being scared."

"What if he does this to her?" I asked.

"I SAID GET OUT AND I MEAN RIGHT NOW! GET YOUR STUFF AND GET OUT OF HERE!"

"Momma would turn over in her grave if she heard this mess that you are doing. You know that we weren't raised like this. YOUR KIDS COME FIRST. YOU KNOW THAT GIRL IS NOT LYING ON HIM. If you keep your eyes closed her sister will be next. He doesn't care because they aren't his kids and once a sick dog, always a sick dog. You gone die with this on your conscience," she said leading me to my room. I packed my things and wept like a baby.

At age 15 I gave birth to a little girl. I named her Flower. She was beautiful and delicate. I continued to stay with my aunt until I was able to get my own section 8 apartment. I guess mom was right. I would never be nothing but a whore on welfare because I got buck wild. I dropped out of school and I had men left and right. I never let them come stay in my home because I would die before anything like what happened to me happen to my Flower. She was so pretty. I was glad she looked nothing like Max. Everyone said she looked like my twin. Mom still won't speak to me. She knows now that I wasn't lying because no sooner than I left he tried to get Peaches', and she blew that whistle. Mom finally put him out. No other men have been in there either. I guess mom is too embarrassed to face me, but I have long gotten over the animosity and ill will that I had for her. I don't understand her rationale, but that is still my mother. She did the best an unreformed alcoholic could do. I guess.

I was getting paid through the state and governmental assistance so I didn't do anything but have a good time with my men and take care of my baby. By the time I decided to get my GED and perhaps a job, I was pregnant again. I did this one on purpose. Well I wasn't trying to get pregnant, but I was doing what it took. It's like Max opened me up to a sex demon or something because I had to have it. It wasn't even good to me, but my body craved it. I also liked the attention I got. I was cute and men wanted me and I wanted them. I had no one to answer to so I did it just to do it. I smoked weed, drank beer, partied, and had my men. I wasn't then and am currently not sure of who my son's father is. I named him Jamel. He looked nothing like me. He looked like my boyfriend Mike when he was first born, but as the days went by, he looked more like Tony my, other little friend. Neither of them was the wiser. My check increased and I put off getting my GED. My rent was all of 15 dollars a month, and I got food stamps. I didn't need anything else. I did want to get out of the projects because there were drugs, gangs, and shoot-outs all around. This was all I knew. I didn't know how I would survive now with two kids living outside of the projects. With in the next two years I was pregnant again. I gave birth to a little girl. I named her Jashaunna. I knew her dad very well. As a matter of fact I did slow down and get one man. He didn't live with us, but he was around a lot. He was a street pharmacist, or in laymen's terms, a drug dealer. He eventually got himself in a lot of mess and now is in jail for a long time.

Jashaunna and Flower look like they could be twins if it weren't for the age difference. They both looked just like me. One day my sister Peaches came over and she encouraged me to get my GED. She had it going on. She got a scholarship and she had a real good job. Beauty and brains -- what more did she need. She had her

own place and no kids. That's the only
thing I envied about her. I felt
trapped because I was 23 years old, no
high school diploma, and three
children, all with different fathers.
Not to mentioned the two abortions that
I had after Flower was born. If the
truth were to be told I didn't deserve
any better than what I got. Peaches
deserved it. I messed up at 14 getting
pregnant by my mom's live-in boyfriend.
Stupid me.

"Girl why do you think like that?
That's what's gonna keep you here. My
nieces and nephew deserve the best and
so do you. I am no different than you
are."

"What can I do besides work at a
fast food place?"

"Girl, we are going to first work
on your GED. Then I can get you on
this program that does training with
computers. Your training is for six
weeks and then you begin working. You
are actually paid for training. The
best thing is that it is state owned
and they offer employees free childcare
during training. So what do you
think?" she asked.

"I don't know," I said hesitantly.

"Well, let's do first things
first."
I got my GED and am now in training
classes. Since I began hanging with my
sister, I hadn't even been dating. I
had a new outlook. I just wanted to
get out of the projects and get a nice

place for my kids to stay. I wanted to
stand on my own two feet once I knew
that it was possible. One evening I
was on my way to pick up my kids after
class and this man was just standing
there watching me.

"Can I help you?" I asked
harshly.

"Yes you can. I have been
noticing you. I was wondering if you
would be free for dinner?" he asked
very self-assuredly.

"I don't even know you."

"My name is Steve. What's your
name?"

"Look, I am not trying to be rude,
but I am not interested in dating right
now. My mind is on one track, and you
wouldn't be interested in dealing with
someone like me. Anyway I am not into
men right now. My priorities are much
different. Sorry." I picked up my
books and started walking toward the
door.

"I can appreciate your honesty. I
didn't ask to marry you or anything. I
just wanted to know your name and ask
if you wanted to eat something so I
could join you."

"I really have to go. Maybe
another time, but not now."

"What's your name?"

"Yvette. My name is Yvette
Anderson."

"I am Steven Parker, and it is
more than a pleasure to meet you."

He had the most radiant smile. He was
simply gorgeous and ordinarily I
would've been trying to get with him
too, but it was a new day. "OK. It's
nice to meet you too."

"Let's say tomorrow we go and get
something to eat?"

"I realize that you are confident,
but I am afraid that you are deaf. I
don't have time and neither do I want
to go to eat with you."

"All right. I'll just come back
another day and we'll go when you are
in a better mood."

"Why are you following me?"

"I am just walking you to your
car."

"See, you know you are wrong. I
don't have a car."

"Oh that's funny? He asked.

"Well check this out. Do you need
a ride?"

"I am going to pick up my children
and then I am catching the bus home."

"I am serious. A beautiful woman
like you doesn't need to be out here
catching the bus with kids. No. Now I
am putting my foot down. I'll at least
drive you to the bus station."

"Fine." I really didn't want to
walk two miles tonight to catch the
bus. He walked with me to the daycare
center and then went to get the car
while I checked the kids out. I had to
give it to Steve, he was very
persistent. He was more fine than
persistent, but I knew that I had to

stay focused and that he wasn't going
to be interested in my kids. He ended
up taking us all the way home. I was
so ashamed because I knew that he
didn't live in the projects. He made
it seem like nothing, but I know he was
like "I can't talk to her now." Maybe
I should've just said no.

The very next day like clockwork
he was there. "How are you today?"
I was shocked he came by. "I am doing
fine. Thank you for the ride
yesterday. I really appreciated that."

"It was more than my pleasure.
Tonight what do you think about
dinner?"

"Steve, it was a really nice
gesture, you taking me home and all. I
just don't want anything more right
now."

"What? You're not going to eat
tonight? That's all that I am asking.
I want to be able to eat dinner tonight
and look into the face of a beautiful
woman." He got straight up serious
with me.

"This beautiful woman has three
small children and they eat too."

"That's a given. If I take you, I
know that your children will be there.
If I had a problem with that then I
would not have even asked you. So what
do you think?"

"Where are you thinking of taking
us on a night like this?"

"Actually I was going to ask you
what did you think about us grabbing

some fast food for the kids and letting my daughter Tracey stay at your house with them. Then you and I would go to dinner. That way they won't have to be out too late."

Tracey was his 16-year-old daughter. I met her the previous night. Steve had been divorced for 12 years. He and his ex-wife were still friends. He said that they married really early. She had been remarried for a while. He didn't say whether she had other children. He didn't say much about anything. He just asked a lot of questions about me. Tracey stayed with him during the week to go to the School of the Arts. Steve said that she was a very talented dancer and singer.

"That's a nice gesture, but the kids don't know her, it's a school night, and Tracey has to go to bed too. Plus my house is a mess."

"You have an excuse for everything. What about us going out on Friday night? That's my last and final offer."

"Yes. I'll go."

"What? Good."

"I'll see if my sister will keep my kids, and if she is unavailable, then Tracey can stay." We both agreed.

Peaches kept a hectic schedule and wasn't available to keep the kids. Tracey was very enthusiastic about keeping them. Classes were closed on Fridays so we met at my house. He told me to dress up. I wasn't for all of

that, but I did it. They showed up
about 8:00 p.m.

"Hey Miss Yvette," Tracey said.

"Hey Miss Tracey. You guys come
in. It's not much, but it's ours until
we can do better."

"It's beautiful in here," she
said.

"Well, the kids are in the back
room watching television. I left money
and coupons on the kitchen counter so
you can order y'all a pizza. Emergency
numbers are on the refrigerator. Ok
that's all."

"You don't have anything to worry
about. My mom has two small children
too, and I am an expert on childcare,"
Tracey said.

"O. K. I'm gone. Mommy loves you
guys. Be good!" I yelled.

"Bye mommy," they said together.

"Have fun mommy. I love you,"
Flower said running into the living
room and kissing my cheek.

"I love you, too baby." I picked
her up to hug her. She and I had
always had this bond with each other.
I was a little partial to her at times
because of what we both went through
with my mother and Max. I believed
that your baby goes through what you do
when you are pregnant. I still make
sure that I treat them the same and
give them all the attention that they
need.

"Are you ready?" Steve asked.

"Yes."

"You look gorgeous."
This man was simply gorgeous himself.
I wasn't about to tell him that. I'm
not even supposed to be interested in
him. "Thank you."

"All right. You be good Tracey.
We'll see you in a little while."
He pulled the door closed. We went to
this fancy seafood restaurant. It
overlooked the river, and we could see
the moon's reflection off of the water.
The view was beautiful, almost
breathtaking. The restaurant was small
and intimate. It was lit only with
candles and a few lights by the exit.

I was really hungry and ate fish,
crab, shrimp, and lobster. This place
was expensive, but their portions were
enormous. I had to get a doggy bag,
and so did he. Steve shocked me. He
was actually rather quiet at dinner.
We did some small talk, but nothing in
depth until we walked around the port
of the river. It was cool and breezy.
You could smell the calmness in the
air. He could tell that I was chilly
by the way I was rubbing my arms. He
took off his jacket and put it on me.

"Can I hold your hand?" he asked.

"Yes. Why are *you* so quiet
tonight? I practically have to cover
your mouth to keep you quiet."

"There is nothing wrong. I am
just really happy being here with you
tonight and I didn't want to say
anything wrong to mess up this mood."

"What mood?"

"You have been smiling all night and you are so beautiful that I don't want to say or do anything to take away that expression on your face."

"That's sweet. I am not a mean woman, Steve. I have just been through so much. I am only 24 and I am really trying to get my life together. I know that you are much older than I am and I don't want to waste your time."

"Hey. I am not *that* much older than you are. I am only six years your senior. Age is nothing but a number to me. I have been through a lot too. Yvette, I don't want anything from you." He pulled me to him and looked directly into my eyes. "I want to be able to make you smile and keep you smiling. I feel your heart. You have built up walls to protect yourself from more hurt and I understand that. It's not me that you are protecting yourself from. I am strong enough to stand and crush the walls that you have built. I have not been with a lot of women, but I have been with enough to know damaged goods. I'm here to be your healer. I don't want to be held I want to hold you. I don't need to be loved I love myself so now I can love you. I am only here to make your life easy. I'm your genie. Your wish is my command."

"Well, dang. I've got to give it too you. You have a strong game," I said laughing.

"Games are for kids, and that, I am not. I am as serious as a heart

attack. You'll see. Time has a way of
revealing all truth. That's all I have
is time," he said looking up at the
stars.

   We continued to walk and then we
went to this coffeehouse for desert.
He told me about his relationship with
his daughter. He said that her mom
allowed her to spend so much time with
him because she didn't want Tracey to
resent the other two kids for their
relationship with their dad. She just
recently started spending the week with
him and the weekend at her moms. He
asked me about my children's father,
and that's when I got uncomfortable. I
refused to lie but I didn't want to
discuss any of that.

   "Jashaunna's father is in jail for
drugs and a lot of other illegal stuff.
Jamel's dad is God knows where. I
would have to write a book to tell
about Flower's dad. I guess you are
looking at me thinking 'all her kids
got different dads.' Huh?"

   "I can tell you are not a mind
reader. I was thinking how beautiful
you are. Then I asked myself didn't
the men in your past see the jewel
inside of you. Then I thought how
lucky I am that they were blind and
that I can see."

   We left there and he brought me
home. I just knew that he would be
trying to make advances, but he didn't.
As a matter of fact he only kissed me
lightly on my cheek. By this time I

wanted this man to do more than kiss
me. His sincerity drove me to the
point of true admiration for him. He
had a way of making words come alive.
He reminded me of a poet or a
philosopher. When I got in my house it
smelled so fresh like bleach and pines.
The clothes that I had in the washer
and dryer were folded and neatly in the
baskets. All of my dishes were put
away. Tracey had bathed the kids and
put them to bed. She fell asleep in my
bed. I was out done. I was ready for
them to move in. This had to have been
a dream. I exchanged numbers with
Steve and they left.

We continued to go out and he
remained a gentleman. Sometimes I
wanted him to be a bad boy, but he kept
his cool. I did eventually tell him
about what happened to me as a child
and he never changed. I was ready to
go further in our relationship, but he
was slow and steady. Not only was he a
charmer with his looks and eloquent
speech, but the man could cook too. He
finally invited me to his house one
Sunday evening for dinner. He had
Luther on the stereo, candles
everywhere, and put roses in my hands.
He baked pork chops in a tomato base,
smothered with onions, peppers,
mushrooms, and topped with mozzarella
cheese, on a bed of rice. He had the
prettiest tossed salad with the works,
and dinner rolls. We drank some
sparkling grape juice because he didn't

drink. After dinner we toured his
elaborate home. There were three
bedrooms, 2 1/2 bathrooms, and a fully
finished basement with an entertainment
room. We watched a movie, and he
asked me what I thought of marriage. I
told him I never thought that anyone
would be interested. We talked a
little more then kissed. I found out
what he was made of. I had never been
touched like that in all of my life.
His hands felt like a feather. His
lips were so smooth, like rose petals.
The ripples in his body glistened in
the candlelight from the oils of
perspiration that came from his body.
He kissed me from head to toe. He
didn't leave a fold or crease of my
body untouched. He actually kissed my
eyebrows. This man had proven to me
that talk is cheap and it's not what
you say it's what you do. He did it
well.

On my 25th birthday he proposed to
me. I said yes. He was crazy about my
kids, and they were crazy about him.
He asked me where I wanted our ceremony
to be. Ironically enough there was
this big church in the heart of
downtown that I used to fantasize about
having my dream wedding. We went to
see what the requirements would be to
use the church. I thought it would be
simple, but there were quite a few
things we had to do.

Besides the fees we had to go
through counseling for six weeks and,

if we were not born again, we had to
give our lives to Christ. No one had
every offered Christ to me. I always
thought that Christians were holy
rollers or something. The preacher
never mentioned us rolling, just
confessing our sins, and I had a lot of
them. The preacher said that I didn't
have to verbally say each sin I had
done, but to generally admit to
sinning, and God would forgive me. We
actually started attending the church
and joined before we got married. We
never went to church when I was a child
except on Easter. During the next few
months my life changed. I became a
Christian, I was engaged to a knight in
shining armor, and I became a working
woman and got out of the projects.

   We had a lovely wedding in the
church of my dreams. I don't think
over 50 people attended, but it was
beautiful. It didn't matter to me if
it was just Steve, the preacher, and
me. I was just overjoyed to be his
wife. Within the course of a year I
was pregnant again. This was a happy
occasion. I made Peaches the
Godmother/auntie of this baby. Peaches
gave her life to Christ also. I was
never able to give her anything in
life. As a matter of fact she'd always
seemed like the big sister. When I
found out about Jesus I had to
introduce them. We both joined the
choir. Tracey was even on their dance
ministry team. Steve became a big

brother, and my mom even accepted
Christ. She did not join any
auxiliaries, but she was connected to
the body and that's all that matters.

Auntie Queeta comes from time to
time, but she had issues that go way
back. Pastor Sampson said we had to
pray for those blinded by Satan, and
that one day, they would believe.

I was shocked when I went into
labor and found out that I was pregnant
with twins. Two girls that we named
Love and Hope. This is what God gave
to me. I thought that I would never be
anything or anybody, but He gave me
Love through people and Hope to keep on
living despite the odds. Now I have
Flower, Jamel, Jashaunna, Love, and
Hope. With Christ as the head of our
lives, we all have Joy.

Chapter Five

VARCELLE

"Little miss perfect, little miss prissy, little miss whatever." If I've heard it once, I've heard it a thousand times. Everyone always thought I was so pretty, so smart, so perfect, and to me, I was none of that. I always found myself trying to live up to other's expectations but on the inside I felt so empty. People were always around me and always wanted me around, but I was so unhappy. I have never really known who I was. I was what my family and friends wanted me to be. I felt like I was living a lie -- actually, I was. No one knew the real Varcelle Robinson. My life was a lie. Living two lives has never been simple, but somehow I managed and was never discovered. Well, not until I came clean. I don't remember when I started having feelings for women, but I do remember wishing that I could just be honest and be accepted, which wasn't happening. I am the oldest of four children with two brothers and one sister. We are all two years apart. My parents planned it that way and so it was. Everything in my life had to be perfect. I am sure this is the reason that I have never told anyone. Who would I tell? My dad was one of the most popular pastors in

the city, Bishop Leroy Robinson. Who
hasn't seen him on television, heard
him on radio, or perhaps just read one
of his books?   My mom was the perfect
first lady. Always dressed for the
occasion, always humbly submissive, and
always right by his side. We had
several pieces of land all over the
United States. I can't remember ever
wanting for anything. We all had our
own bedrooms, and I never had to share
anything. We didn't wear hand-me-
downs, and frankly I rather enjoyed
that part of my life. I hated the fact
of never being able to bring home less
than an "A" without being put on
punishment. The Robinson name was one
that couldn't be tarnished, and anyone
that jeopardized it would feel the
wrath of Leroy, Sr.

There was nothing humble about
daddy so I could never share with him
what I was going through in my heart
and mind. Mom always sided with him
even when she knew he was wrong so I
couldn't trust her. My brothers,
sister, and I weren't close -- well in
public we were. I had to be the
"example" so there was no sharing with
them.

A female first approached me when
I was in seventh grade. It was after
gym class, and we had to shower before
the next class period. I was the last
to come out and this girl named Shelly
was in the locker room. Shelly was
about 16, but she had been kept back a

few times. She would always wait for
me, and I intentionally would try to
come out last so that no one would see
me. Somehow she always managed to be
last too. To look at her you would
never know that she was gay. She was
just as "prissy" as I was. I had a so-
called boyfriend, but it was just
because that was what I was supposed to
do. I still, to this day, don't know
what attracted me to women. I was
never molested, to my knowledge. All I
know is that I have always been
intrigued and Shelly brought it out of
me. Since I was a strait "A" student
she asked me to tutor her. That was
what she wanted on the surface, but her
goal was to turn me out. Because of
her middle class status, my parents had
no problems with me riding to school
with her, going to her house, and even
spending the night. She never
approached me from the start, but
gradually introduced me to lesbianism.
It started off with talks about sex and
pregnancy. That was an issue in middle
school because there were so many
pregnant girls or ones that already had
children. Shelly said that she would
never have kids and that there was only
one way to guarantee that she would not
get pregnant and that was to not have
sex with boys. She taught me about my
body and how women are sexually
aroused. She would tell me what was
supposed to happen after women were
turned on and what the men should do.

She then schooled me on the alternative
methods of sexual satisfaction. She
had so many books, a borderline "D"
student at school, but a whiz kid when
it came to sex. She had my curiosity
going to the maximum. We went from
sex 101 to watching movies that were
XXX rated. Can you imagine being 13
and being exposed to this type of
drama? Well, I was. Her mom didn't
know she was at work all of the time.
Her dad did send her money, but they
lived in the same neighborhood that we
lived in and it cost a little bit more
than minimum wages to live there.

My body had just started
developing. I had breast, hips, and
pubic hairs, but I still hadn't started
my period. This was all new to me. I
knew it was wrong, but I was drawn to
it. I still had my little boyfriend,
but at my age there was no serious
dating going on. There were just
little boys who thought that you were
cute and wanted to "go with you". They
had no car, no money, maybe a small
kiss behind the building from time to
time. They could forget coming to my
house. Leroy would kill them for even
calling. I could forget dating. I was
too young anyway.

Shelley and I eventually graduated
to the next level and that's what got
me hooked. After the first encounter,
I didn't want to anymore. Well, my
mind didn't. My body hungered for her.
It got to the point where she showed me

how to get that satisfied feeling even when she wasn't around. By the time I was in high school, we had begun to recruit other girls. It was our secret though. It's easier to tell when a guy was gay than it is with a girl. There were only four of us that hung together all of the time, but we were couples. We all had boyfriends, well except one of the girls. She was out of the closet. She looked like a dude too. People would ask us how could we be friends with her. Little did they know that we were "family".

Shelly was becoming a bit possessive. By the time I was senior, I was so active in extra curricular activities that I didn't have much time for her. I had a boyfriend that was popular, I was on varsity cheerleading for football and basketball. I was president of student council, vice president of the drama team, and I was still the preacher's daughter at church. Shelly really showed her true colors on the night of the coronation. I was homecoming queen and even I have to admit I looked beautiful.

"So where are we going after this thing is over with?" she asked.

"This thing is a very important event to me. As far as I know I am going to be with Keith afterwards."

"You are always with him. What's up with that? We haven't been together in a while."

"But you know that I have a boyfriend. It's not like you and I go together. I thought we had an understanding."

"Still, you know what time it is? Oh, so Miss Perfect done forgot about her little secret, huh?"

"You are wrong for that. How can you throw that up in my face? I didn't ask for this you know. You came to me."

"Yeah, well maybe I did, but we have been "family" for some years and now that you got some boyfriend you ain't got no time for me," she said starting to get loud.

"Lower your voice. There are people in the other dressing rooms."

"What do you have to hide? You can't keep avoiding me."

"I am not avoiding you. I just need some space. This is too much right now. We will always be friends. True friends understand when other friends need space."

"No. What I understand is that you're scared that you're going to be found out and you're trying to hide."

"Of course I don't want anyone to know about this. Are you crazy?"

"Are you and Keith having sex?"

"Why are you asking me this and why now? I don't belong to you. That is not the topic of discussion anyway."

"Well, let's change the subject. Answer the question."

"I really would like it if you would leave. I will call you later. I promise."

"Just forget it. Don't call. It's over," she said walking over to the door.

"What do you mean over? Friendship doesn't stop over petty junk like this."

"To you it's petty, and to me it's urgent. I see where I stand."

I couldn't believe that she was serious. I know that I had been busy, but I didn't think she would trip out like this. I knew I had to talk to her because my life couldn't revolve around her. Maybe this was for the best. She was serious. She said that she was not about to be there just for my convenience. We still saw each other from time to time, but the less I saw of her, the less I needed to see her. I actually thought that I was over women. Maybe it was just a phase. I was not gay. Good.

Keith and I were sleeping together, but not often. I didn't get anything out of it. Sometimes I would want to give Keith a crash course in sex 101. He was a good kisser, but it was wham bam thank you ma'am. Keith and I stayed together until the fall after graduation. We broke up because we were both going to college out of town, and didn't want to do the long distance thing. There wasn't much love lost. We liked one another but I think

it was the fact that we were so popular
and it seemed right at the time. I
went away to college and I met a slew
of men. I was cool though. Most of
the guys were really just my friends.
I became an AKA, was on the dean's list
every semester, and graduated at the
top of my class. Yes, I was
valedictorian. I received my B.S. in
Psychology.

I went through college with no
lesbian experiences. I knew that I was
cured. Although my thoughts would
travel there, and I would dream of it,
I felt that if I wasn't practicing, I
was all right. I did fall in love with
this hunk of chocolate named Andre. He
was from a very well to do family. We
dated for a short while and became
involved sexually. I enjoyed sex with
him. I think he went to "Shelly's
school of intimacy". I got engaged
during my junior year and we got
married the summer after I graduated.
There were over 500 people there.
These were basically people that my
parents knew. The local news even
covered the event. It was exciting
with video cameras everywhere. The
scene was like a botanical garden with
all of the flowers. The weather was
perfect and sunny, only about 80
degrees with a light breeze from time
to time. I felt like a princess. I
was a June bride with many issues, but
this was my day. Guess who was there?
Shelly.

I felt like all that was in me would sink in my stomach when I saw her. She played it cool and actually got us a gift. This was a day that I'd never forget. I felt like a celebrity, and for the most part, I was. We were actually featured on a show that does exclusives on weddings and receptions. I felt like Cinderella when she married her prince.

That fall I stayed in the city and went to graduate school to get my Ph.D. in Psychology. My husband was CEO at his father's business. They had four McDonald's franchises all over the city. Business was really booming for them. We both stayed busy with life and church and always had time to date. He was the only guy that made me feel half as good as Shelly made me feel. I would try to get her out of my system, but whenever I went to bed with Andre she was there, especially the times that it was good. I still didn't think that I was gay anymore. I didn't have any desire for women like I did when I was younger. I still thought about it from time to time, but Dre kept my mind occupied enough to not wonder off. As time went on, I got pregnant during my third year of graduate school. I had a little boy whose name was Andre, Jr. of course. He was the first grandchild on both sides of our family so you know that he was spoiled rotten. After I had him everyone started drinking that water. My sister Victoria, who is

married, had twins the next year. Both
of my brothers are married too. Leroy
Jr., the one under me, has a daughter.
My brother Victor has two daughters
that weren't twins, but were about 11
months apart. After I received my
Ph.D. I got pregnant again. I had
another boy. We were hoping for a
girl, but God blessed us with a boy
named Antonio. I had my tubes tied
because we only wanted two children and
that was it. With my happy family, I
was so miserable. I had a monster of a
secret on the inside that I could never
get rid of. As a child, parents
provide assurance that monsters were a
figment of the imagination, but my
monster was alive and waiting for a
chance to kill me.

Andre's best friend and his wife
hit some hard times and they lost their
home. I was hesitant at first, but we
decided to let them stay with us until
they got back on their feet. We had a
program at church for families like
them, but this was "Dre's boy". Since
they didn't have any children it made
it easy. Andre's friend's name was
Travis and his wife's name was Brenda.
They were really sweet. She was rather
timid, but seemed to be one that would
try not to be shy so that Travis
wouldn't trip -- Travis was an
extravert. I could tell that she lived
in his shadow. People would refer to
her as Travis's wife or lady. I lived
in no one's shadow. I was Dr. Varcelle

Robinson-Harris, Ph.D. There I was
working with mentally ill patients
daily. Diagnosing their problems and
knowing what type of behavior they were
displaying, but there was nothing I
could do for my skeletons. I just
wanted to see if I was gay. I'd say
that I wasn't time after time, but
there was still something in me that
cried out for a women. No money,
prestige, or amount of degrees pacified
the longing I had to be free. Even at
church they talked about homosexuality,
adultery, and fornication, but I never
felt like anything applied to me. They
preached hell fire and brimstone, but I
still felt like I needed help. No one
could discern what I was going through.
I was saved and I had the Holy Ghost (I
thought), but I was constantly
wrestling. The older I got and the
more I obtained materialistically, the
more I needed to be free. My secret
held me captive and no one knew but
God. I guess.

"We really appreciate you guys
letting us stay with you. Whatever you
need me to do just let me know," Brenda
said.

"Girl, don't worry about anything.
Whatever your hands find to do help
yourself. Sometimes I do need a hand
with the kids, but normally their nanny
takes care of the necessities."

"How does it feel being a big time
doctor?"

"Girl, please. I am not big time, yet." We laughed.

"Sometimes I feel like I need a psychiatrist."

"Girl, you are so funny."

"No. I am serious. I have a lot in me and nobody to talk to."

"Well, you can talk to me. I don't have any friends." Everything always centers on Travis. I have to be his everything. He is so jealous that he wouldn't allow me to have many girlfriends or even go anywhere without him. What I am saying is that you can trust me. Who would I tell? Are you having marital problems or what?"

"No. I don't want to burden you with my issues. I believe that I can trust you, but you wouldn't begin to understand?"

"Try me."

"My problem is with my feelings. I don't know what I feel or how I should feel."

"I'm feeling you." We laughed. "No. I am serious I understand what you are not saying."

"I've been holding this in since I was a child. I could never tell anyone. Everybody always expected the best out of me. I can't do this," I said shaking my head.

"Come on. We live in the same house. Why can't we act like family?"

"I think that is the problem. I can't tell family. I can't tell anyone

not even you," I said going into the
other room.

"Wait Varcelle. Don't do this.
Everybody needs someone. I am here for
you, girl," she said reaching to hug
me.

As we embraced I felt something.
Something I hadn't felt in years. It
was almost as if she knew, but was
waiting for me to say it to her. I
abruptly let go.

"What's wrong?" she asked looking
confused.

"Nothing. I just want to be alone
right now."

"O. K. I am here if you need me."

That was weird. I hadn't felt
like that since Shelly used to hold me.
Surely she couldn't be like me. She
was married, but so was I. Maybe it
was just in my mind.

One night my sister had my kids,
and Dre and Travis were at a men's
meeting at church. Brenda came in my
room, and I felt that feeling again. I
would only feel it when she and I were
alone.

"Can you, well do you feel up to
talking?" she asked.

"I was kind of tired, but what's
up?"

"I've been feeling like you don't
want to be around me. Are we out
wearing our welcome?"

"Oh, no! Girl, I just have a lot
on my mind. I wish you could imagine
what I am dealing with. They just

nominated me to be over the young women's department in our church. I don't have the time nor am I equipped to do this. I feel like I am being set up. Never mind. I really don't feel like talking."

"Fine. You don't have to. You are so tense. Just relax and let me give you a massage. That's what I do for a living anyway."

"Why not?" I thought.

I turned over and she began. At first it was nice. After a while it was still nice, but a different kind of nice. Brenda wasn't a Christian although she went to church with us. I felt something in me saying, "this is enough, STOP!" However, I didn't move when I heard the voice. She began to turn me on, and I know she knew it. She began kissing on me. I wanted to stop her, but my body wanted it. Everything in me knew that this was wrong, but I went along with it. I knew she was "family". That's the term Shelly said we'd use to say that someone was gay. Something in me knew, but now I was sure. After that night I didn't want to look anyone in the face. As a matter of fact I cancelled all of my appointments for the day. Here I go again. What should I do? Now I have defiled my marriage and the guilt was unimaginable. They had to leave our house. What would I say to Andre? If they stayed she could either tell or this may be an ongoing affair. I

couldn't have that in front of my kids
in my home that my husband and I
shared. What is wrong with me?

Brenda and I talked and we vowed
never to tell anyone. She said that
was not an option anyway. We also
vowed to never let that happen again,
and it didn't. I prayed and asked God
to forgive me, but I still had this
issue. What would happen the next time
that I was confronted with a
compromising situation? I didn't want
to be a hypocrite, but that is what I
was. I wasn't being real. Who could I
possibly get deliverance from in the
church? Everyone would be judgmental
or breech confidentiality. We would
even have women's meetings at the
church. I mean we would go deep.
Women would confess everything from
wanting to commit adultery to admitting
to being molested as kids, being
battered, and even having their
husbands cheating on them. No one ever
had a lesbian experience or thought of
it. It never even came up. Who could
I confide in? I needed deliverance. I
didn't like the fact of me praying over
people and seeing them delivered when
all the time I was trapped in this
shell. I didn't even understand how or
why God would use me to minister to
anyone. It was one thing to do it in
the work field, that's what I went to
school for. It was a bit much helping
and ministering in the church. I
wanted to break out but how? One day I

went to a Women's retreat and this lady
called me out. She told me to read
Exodus 3:8,9 and that I would find what
I was searching for.

Exodus 3:8 and 9 says, "And I am
come down to deliver them out of the
hand of the Egyptians, and to bring
them up out of that land unto a good
land and a large, unto a land flowing
with milk and honey; unto the place of
the Canaanites, and the Hittites, and
the Amorites, and the Perizzites, and
the Hivites, and the Jebusites. (9) Now
therefore, behold, the cry of the
children of Israel is come unto me: and
I have also seen the oppression
wherewith the Egyptians oppress them."

I read it, but I still felt bound.
Then one day I went to a "Women Thou
art Set Free" conference. During one
of the morning sessions it came out.
The speaker was awesome. This
particular part of the conference was
not televised. The speaker wasn't even
well known. That didn't matter because
she knew God and he sent her to deliver
me. Once you've been bound for so long
it doesn't matter who your deliverer
is, you just want help to get free.
Her scripture text came from Exodus
3:8,9 and her topic was "Your Deliverer
is Here". She called out every spirit
there was. The thing was we weren't
ashamed so we ran to that altar, and
God did a purging on the inside of me.
Even after I had left, the devil said
that I wasn't free, but I have been

walking in total deliverance ever
since. I no longer battle with the
thought of other women and I don't
dream of women any longer. It has been
over a year, and I have not had a
desire to think of Shelly nor any other
women. I have even been able to share
my testimony and others have come
clean. Shelly and Brenda have given
their lives to the Lord. Now we are
fighting against this spirit together.
My husband still doesn't know, but I am
free and I no longer feel that I am
hiding anything from him. Maybe one
day I will share it, but until God
releases me, it will remain where it
is. It is in the sea of forgetfulness
where God remembers it no more. He has
forgiven me and I am no longer held
hostage to my past. God is able and He
did it just for me.

Chapter Six

MELODY

My motto in life is "NEVER SAY NEVER." I've always had high moral standards. I've never been a super saint. I truly do all that I know to do that is right. I'm not judgmental, but there are some things that are considered TABOO. It is easy to look at a person or a situation and say "if that were me I'd do this or I would never take that". Hypothetically speaking there is a lot we would or would not do. The truth of the matter is until you are in a situation you really don't know what you would do. That's why people that live in glass houses need not throw stones. I started going to church with my best friend, April, when I was 11 years old. I received Christ and began working in the church. I enjoyed it. My family had even started getting involved in church through me. Our church kept the youth busy. We did everything from door to door witnessing, to selling candy, to having talent shows. It was so exciting to the point that I would rather be in church than school. By the time that I was 15 we had kids from the neighborhood, our schools, and even their parents. Our church had grown to

the point that we had to end up
purchasing the property on the entire
block that we were on. People were
coming in by the truckload. We were
not only growing in numbers, but people
were actually giving their lives to the
Lord. We would have disagreements and
spats from time to time. Our pastor
would make us nip stuff in the bud. A
lot of disagreements we handled without
him ever finding out about them. The
Spirit of the Lord would move so
heavily sometimes that people would get
healed and demons were being cast out,
it was like a modern day book of Acts.
Our pastor was a man of great wisdom.
He was so anointed that sometimes we'd
be in service and he'd walk by and
people would fall out and even get
healed. His goal was to make sure that
if nothing else, we knew the word of
God and that we lived it. That way we
could effectively witness and cause
others to be saved. We loved Pastor
Watkins to death. People even said that
we worshiped him. I just think we all
had a high respect and honor for him
because he gave us hope. When I turned
16 we had a special service for our
pastor in honor of his hard labor in
the ministry. I had just done a
musical selection on the saxophone.
Pastor Watkins loved to hear me play.
He always said that I had a special
anointing in my hands.
There was a loud noise on the outside
of the sanctuary. It was so loud that

we could hear it above the music. The
next thing I knew one of the men jumped
on me and yelled, "Don't move!"

All I heard was screams and glass
shattering.

"GET DOWN! EVERYBODY GET DOWN!"
one of the men screamed.

After about 10 minutes of chaos it
was completely silent. The man that
was on me got up and brushed himself
off.

"Are you all right?"

"Yeah. What happened?"

"I don't know." He said.

"Ah! No!" Some woman screamed.

Then there were screams all over.
I jumped up. All I saw was glass and
blood. I got so nauseated. It felt
like a dream. The lights had gone dim
and they were flashing on and off.
One of the ushers ran to the pulpit.
Pastor Watkins had been hit. Once that
was known everybody was going crazy.
He had a smile on his face. I was
shaking and screaming. My sister ran
over to me, and we were holding each
other crying. She was trembling like
a leaf. I brushed the glass off of her
shirt. Everybody was looking for his or
her family member. I had remembered
that my brother was on back door usher
duty. "Where is Chuck?" I thought.
Before I could finish my thought Lisa
hollered.

"Chuck!"

"Where is he?" I asked.

We both ran down the aisle. One of the brothers stopped us.

"You guys can't go back there."

"Why? Where is our brother?"

"We are trying to get things under control. Please have a seat up here for now."

Then I heard what seemed to be thousands of sirens. I couldn't believe that anyone would shoot at a church. What was this world coming to? The police department, ambulance, and even the newscasters were there. Once all was said and done we had 10 people to be killed, seven people critically injured, about four that had minor injuries, and a church full of grieving people. My family was among those grieving for a personal lost. My brother, Charles Lewis Brown better known as "Chuck" at age 19 was shot in the head. The doctors said that he died immediately. Our pastor was numbered among the casualties. I felt so emotionally paralyzed. We had two babies to be killed, a newlywed couple, and my friend April's cousin. This was a tragedy that I would not soon forget. As a result of this, the church was closed down. Of all the people that could've taken over, no one wanted to. I didn't go to anyone else's church after that. I don't know if I was just scared or what. I still loved God, but I didn't want to get close to any other church family the way that I had with Greater Faith. I did keep in touch

with some of the people. As a matter
of fact, I started dating one of the
boys from the church. Carl was about
three years older than I was. Carl was
my first and only real boyfriend. We
helped each other through the tragedy.
It took me a long time to stop dreaming
about it. I still don't think that
there is a day that I don't think about
what happened. I miss my brother
everyday especially on holidays and his
birthday. He was the "class clown".
He always kept us laughing. Life is
not the same without him. Slowly but
surely I am learning to cope. I did
graduate from high school, but instead
of college I decided to work. I worked
at the mall in a department store. I
made a little more than minimum wage.
I had a great schedule. I worked in
the mornings Monday through Friday and
I had weekends off. I still managed to
see Carl everyday. If we weren't on
the phone, we were together. Carl
asked me to marry him and I said yes.
My parents were not cool with it. They
said we could date, but I was too young
to get married.

"She's fresh out of high school.
She doesn't know anything about life
yet. How are you going to take care of
her?" My dad asked.

"We both are working and I already
have my own place. I can take care of
her."

"I say that you all should wait a
few years. Love can wait. What's the

hurry? She's not pregnant is she?" Mom
asked.

"What does pregnancy have to do
with it? That's no reason to get
married," I said.

"Well how about this? Ain't gone
be no marriage as long as I got
something to do with it," Dad said.

We let the conversation end just
like that. Dad was right. If they had
anything to do with it, we wouldn't get
married. So that meant that they
couldn't have anything to do with it.
So we eloped. Yes we did. It was as
simple as pie. The hardest part was
being married and no one finding out.
So I still had a curfew and everything.
I must say it kept things interesting
between us two. I can remember those
nights in my bed without him. I would
be on fire. Carl was my first. I
didn't have anything to compare it to,
but I surely enjoyed what he did and
couldn't wait for him to do it again.
I wanted to tell my sisters, but our
family was too tight. There were no
secrets between us. The only brother I
had was dead, and the ironic thing
about that is I probably would have
told him.

After about three months of hiding
I had to tell. My mom said that she
knew that something fishy was going on.
Dad got over it after about a week.
Carl's family was fine. I moved in
with him and it was divine. With in a
few months I was pregnant. I was sick

as a dog. I couldn't eat, and if
anything had any smell to it I was
vomiting. Once I got around six months
I was better. I was actually more
sexually attracted to Carl at that
stage than ever. He thought that I was
sexy too. Then I started eating
everything in sight. Once I was in my
last trimester I started getting sick
again. I was just ready to get it over
with and be mommy. When that day
finally came I was so energetic. I
rearranged the furniture in the house
and even went walking around at the
mall. I didn't experience the most
excruciating pain until the last stages
of labor I was a miserable soul. Carl
was right there coaching me on. You
would've thought that he was the one
having the baby. He was sweating like
a hog on the hottest summer day. He
was a great coach and if it hadn't been
for him being so patient, I probably
would have screamed. He was so much
fun to be around. Most times it seemed
like he was my friend instead of my
husband. He sometimes reminded me of
my brother. After 19 hours of labor, I
gave birth to a 9 lb., 2oz. baby boy
named Carl Anthony Frazier, Jr. He
looked every bit like Carl. I did the
labor, but he gets the credit for it.
Everybody was crazy about him. My mom
calls him "red". He was adorable. He
had black silky straight hair and the
deepest dark eyes. He was already fat
at two weeks old. He reminded me of a

turkey getting ready to be baked. I couldn't believe that I was a mother. What was I going to teach this little man about life? A lot of people said they didn't want to think of having any more children, especially right after giving birth. I felt differently. The pain was awful, but maybe in another couple of years I'd do it again. Well I got my opportunity much sooner than I expected. I went to visit my doctor because I was experiencing flu like symptoms and guess what? I was 9 weeks pregnant. My baby was only 4 months old. Carl was ok, but I wasn't ready for it. I had to be on bed rest with this pregnancy because I had some major complications. I'd start to spot with the least amount of pressure. I had to keep my legs elevated and do little if any movement. I was in my own little prison. We had to get on welfare to make ends meet because I had to stop working. This brought out another side of Carl. He understood the circumstances, but he hated the situation. He didn't act lovey dovey anymore. Some days he didn't even speak to me. Forget asking how the baby was doing. I was going to all of my check ups alone. By the time I was six months pregnant I hardly saw him at home. He said he was working overtime, but sometimes he would come in long hours after his job was closed. I was highly suspicious. I even asked him if he was cheating and, of course, he said

no. I felt that he was, but I had no
proof. We would even get phone calls
in the middle of the night. If I
answered then they'd hang up. I even
went as far as having my number
changed. Some how they'd end up
calling and hanging up again.

"Carl. I know that we have talked
about this already, but I want to be
assured especially since I am due to
have this baby any day. Is there
another woman?"

"What do you mean? Don't start
this crap. I ain't in the mood!"

"Why are you so defensive? I have
only asked you this once or twice. You
have asked me at least 100 times. I
have never given you a reason to think
that I would cheat. You haven't given
me any reason to think that you aren't,
and I want to be assured."

"My answer has not changed. So
don't ask me again."

"Have you been drinking and
getting high again?"

"Look. You ain't my mom so quit
questioning me."

He pushed me out of his way. His
push almost knocked me breathless. I
grabbed on to the dresser next to me to
keep from falling.

"Don't be pushing on me. What's
wrong with you? You know that I am
pregnant. Have you lost your mind?"

"No, but you done lost yours
yelling at me like you're crazy!"

He slapped me so hard that I fell on
the floor. Then he came over and
punched me like I was a man. I got so
scared that I froze. I wanted to fight
him back but I couldn't. I didn't know
who he was. After he kicked me my
water broke. I was in shock. Everyone
thought it was because of me being in
labor, and I said no different. I
couldn't tell anybody that I got beat
up by my husband. What would they
think? Then they'd expect me to leave
him. I wasn't going to do that, then
my parents would think "see we were
right you all were not ready for
marriage." I didn't want to hear that.
It was my fault anyway. I was
interrogating him and he was already
going through enough. Working over
time and then playing Mr. Mom to C. J.
and doctor to me.   My baby was going
into distress so I had to have an
emergency c-section.   I had another
boy. I named him Craig Edward Frazier.

     I went to my mom's house for a
week because I couldn't do much after
having surgery. Carl couldn't get off,
and I needed help with the kids. I had
no room at home so I went to my mom's
house. I had two babies in pampers and
depression was overwhelming me.
Carl came over one day with his brother
Ray. He had this big bouquet of
flowers with an array of colors. Pink,
red, yellow, even purple flowers were
in the bunch. He was apologizing for
our "little spat" that we had a few

days before. I wasn't glad to see him,
but his brother Ray always brought
sunshine into our lives. Ray and Carl
were about five years apart in age, but
you couldn't tell. Carl always acted
the oldest, however he was the
youngest. Go figure. Ray was very
laid back and didn't say much, When he
did speak, he'd always leave you with a
deep thought. He was cool though. We
could always talk. In fact, he
reminded me of my brother Chuck. Chuck
had a way of making you feel like you
could tell him anything. That's how
Ray was. His name was really Ramón,
but you know how we always give people
a nickname. He was level-headed and I
appreciated him because he gave his
brother some stability -- when and if
he would listen to him. Carl was very
apologetic for the beat down that he
gave me. Carl promised me that he
would never hit me again.

"I am so sorry. You know that I
have just been stressed and yeah I was
drinking that day. I was guilty and
you know what they say 'a hit dog will
holler.' Will you forgive me? I don't
want to lose you."

"I forgive you."

That was the first of many
apologies. He became more and more
abusive. Carl would beat me sometimes,
and I would actually have to go to the
emergency room. The only person that
knew that anything like that had
happened was Ray. I would call him,

and he would come to the hospital. If
Carl had put me out, he would be my
rescuer. My dad would kill him if he
knew, and I don't know why I stayed
knowing that it would probably happen
again. I felt like I had no way out.
Pride kept me on one hand, and on the
other hand, he was the only man that I
had known. Who wants an out-of-work
woman with two children? Fear and
pride are definitely not a good
combination.

One weekend Carl didn't come home
at all. I called Ray, and he said he
hadn't seen or heard from him. We
needed food and my baby needed pampers
-- where was their father? Ray came to
the rescue again.

"I am sorry to keep dragging you
into our drama, but there is no one
else that I can call."

"Don't even think about it. Carl
is like our old man was before he died.
Papa was a rolling stone. Wherever he
laid his hat was his home. You deserve
so much more. I try to talk to that
knucklehead, but he won't listen. If I
had someone like you, as fine as you
are, I wouldn't mistreat them at all."

"It's a shame that he doesn't
realize that I am a good wife. I can't
help that I got pregnant again. It's
not like I did that on my own. How did
your mother handle your father cheating
and beating on her?"

"Mom and pops were common law so
she didn't say much about the other

women. Now when it came to Pop's
hitting, her she took that for a little
bit, but after a while she began to
fight back. Pops had to end up leaving
because somebody was going to end up
dead and he said it wasn't going to be
him."

"I just want to be treated like a
women should be treated. I have given
this man two sons, my soul, and
whatever he wants, if it's in my power,
I am on it."

I broke down crying. Ray grabbed
me and held me. He laid my head on his
chest. Once I gathered myself I looked
at Ray and he was looking into my eyes.
I felt this fluttering in my belly that
was not gas. I let go, but Ray grabbed
me again and this time he kissed me. I
pushed him away, but he came back and
this time I kissed him back. I swear I
didn't plan for this. I wanted it not
from my brother-in-law but from my man.
I needed his attention. I needed to be
loved and I deserved it. Ray had all
of the qualities that Carl was missing
and my body was in heat. It had been
weeks since we had made love. Actually
he was just jumping on me. His goal was
no longer to please me, but to be
pleased. Some nights he wouldn't even
wait until I was ready. I felt like I
was being raped.

Oh my God! I am kissing my brother
in law. What is wrong with me? It
felt so good though. There were
certain rivers Carl and I had never

crossed and I had no idea that some
things were possible, but Ray took me
to a place that I had never been and
didn't want to leave anytime soon.
With Carl being my first, I didn't know
what else to expect. What he did felt
good. I even thought that I had
enjoyed orgasms with Carl, but I never
had one until that night. My body was
numb by the time we were done. I told
my body to move, and it couldn't. We
used no protection, and my kids were
just in the other room. What were we
thinking? Carl could've walked in on
us, and we would've been busted.

"Did you enjoy yourself?"

"I guess I should say no but I
would only be lying. I feel so bad
though. Here I've been accusing him of
doing what I just did. Not only that,
but you are his brother. I am sorry."

"I feel bad about this happening
and Carl being my brother, but I felt
that you deserved some happiness and I
wanted to give it to you. Are you
happy?"

"No. I feel like a tramp. There
is no way to justify what we did. No
matter how good it was."

"Do you want me to leave?"

"No. Yes. I don't know. I am
confused. I would like for you to
stay, but I don't want him to sense
anything between us. You know that
dogs have radar for mess."

"He won't. No one ever has to
know unless you tell, and since I have

been your confidant, we don't have that to worry about it. I must admit it made me feel good to see your body tremble like you were melting. There's nothing like a satisfied woman."

"That is enough. No more conversation about that." I turned away because of my embarrassment. We went on as if nothing had happened. About two months later we had my son Craig's 3rd birthday party, and I got sick as a dog. Since it was winter I thought maybe I had the flu. A whole lot of people had been getting viruses so perhaps that was my case. After I had been throwing up all day I got a fever and was dehydrated. My mom took me to the emergency room because my temperature was over 103. They ran tests and gave me an I.V.

"Where did Carl go? He was right behind us," Mom asked.

"I guess he'll be here. He probably was making sure that the boys were all right." I knew it wasn't the truth. He was so low down that any chance he got he was with that other woman. I could never do that to a married woman knowing that they have a family and keep her man away. It seems that women would be empathetic knowing how it feels to be cheated on. Women know how other women think. I know what I did with Ray was wrong, but he *is* single. I am not trying to take a married man from anyone.

"Mrs. Frazier I have some good news and then more good news, I hope," The doctor said.

"Well give me the good news."

"You do not have the flu and you are pregnant. You seem to be about seven weeks. You need to get to your gynecologist on Monday morning so you can start your prenatal care."

"I'm gonna have another grandbaby Claude ha' mercy."

I just stared into space for a few minutes. I couldn't respond. Although no one knew what had happened with Ray I knew, and once again my guilt and shame was overwhelming. Carl and I hadn't done anything in I know a good two to three months. That can only mean one thing. Ray. I never really thought that I would even get pregnant. Maybe Carl wasn't keeping up with our encounters and he wouldn't think about it. I almost felt like David in the Bible. When I got home surprisingly Carl was home with the boys.

"Are you ok?" he asked pulling me to him to hug me.

"Doing great!" Mom said.

"What did I miss?"

"I'll let Melody tell you."

"You seemed to be doing a pretty good job with talking Mom."

"What's going on y'all?"

"I am not sick. Put it this way, you're going to be a daddy again."

"Good. These boys are getting rusty anyway. It would be nice to have another baby. Maybe we'll have a girl this time." He really seemed excited and happy.

"You're not glad?" he asked.

"I just wasn't expecting this now," I said hoping that he couldn't feel my vibes of guilt.

"We will be just fine."

When I told Ray he said it would remain his secret, and I said the same.

"Awe man. I never thought you would get pregnant. Seeing how we didn't use anything it is definitely possible."

"I am so ashamed of myself."

"I should be the one ashamed. I mean that is my brother, but you needed me, and I was what you needed at that time. I really feel bad, but there is nothing that I can do to change the past. I am sorry that I over stepped my boundaries as your confidant and brother. I only wanted to make you feel good like any woman should."

"Well you did more than make me feel good. You got me pregnant."

Carl actually started acting like the Carl that I knew before. We were getting along fine. Every blue moon we'd get a phone call that would just hang up, but other than that, we were doing well. We wanted to be surprised so I didn't get an ultrasound to find out the sex of the baby. I went into labor on the fourth of July. I was only in labor for 3 hours and gave birth to another little boy. We named

him Cedric Ramón. Ramón was actually
Carl's idea. I just let it be. Carl
and Ray looked so much alike that it
wasn't strange that the baby favored
Ray or anyone in their family. People
would mistake them for twins sometimes.
When I got home from that hospital it
looked like a storm had gone threw it.
I couldn't believe that Carl didn't at
least try to clean up for us. Toys and
trash decorated my kitchen. While
clean and dirty clothes were the design
in our bedroom. I didn't say a thing.
Once I went into our bedroom I sat on
the bed. I was disgusted. I began
looking around and just had to clean up
a little. As I was placing the clothes
in the hamper, I noticed an unfamiliar
piece of clothing. When I picked it up
I knew it didn't belong to anyone in
the house. I knew what my panties
looked like and these were not them. I
was allergic to silk and I wasn't into
see through clothes. I was rather shy
when it came to lingerie. Carl walked
in.

"Girl, sit down. I'll pick up
these clothes. Don't you do nothing."

"Carl, whose panties are these?"
I asked holding them in the air on one
finger.

"Yours I guess. They're not
mine," he said laughing.

"It's not funny these are not
mine. Who has been in my house?
Forget my house in my bedroom? So now
I am supposed to be stupid? I don't

wear silk underwear and I know what I
wear and these aren't mine."
    "I am sick of this you have
accused me for the last time."
He hit me and it was on. We were
fighting -- yes, I had just had a baby,
but I was tired of being beat up. He
was going to remember that he was in a
fight. For each punch he threw one
came right back at him. I ended up
back in the hospital that same day.
This time I couldn't hide from mom.
She was so mad she was smoking. Her
face was literally red. My jaw was
cracked and he knocked out four of my
front top teeth. I had to end up
getting a partial plate in the front of
my mouth. I decided those things
between Carl and I were not going to
change. I told mom that he had been
beating me since my first baby C. J.
was born. She was hurt that I hid all
of this for so long. I filed for
divorce, and he didn't fight it. He
was cool as long as he could see his
kids. I still don't know who that
other woman was, but I had to go on
with my life. If I didn't have the
kids, it would be easier, but I refused
to leave my kids motherless. I would
rather be lonely than to be dead.
    After the divorce I went back home
with my mother. It was temporary until
I could get a place of my own. My dad
never said I told you so, but I know he
wanted to. My family was very
supportive, and I needed that during

this crazy time in my life. I
eventually got my own place and was
able to get a small car. Although I
was still getting assistance from the
government and child support, I still
had to work overtime. My mom kept my
boys, and I wouldn't dare have her do
it for free. I was an assistant
manager at a grocery store. I liked it
since I was a people person.

What I really missed was playing
the saxophone. I hadn't played since
Pastor Watkins was killed. I always
thought that I would make it big as a
musician. I loved music, but it had
been so long since I played. I didn't
know whether I remembered how to play
or not. One night after I had got home
from work I went into my trunk in my
bedroom and took out my saxophone. I
cleaned it off and tried to tune it up.
I began playing. It all came back to
me. I just broke down and cried. It
brought back too many bad memories. I
had memories of the shoot out, of my
infidelity, and of my divorce. I
missed my husband and being married. I
know that everyday wasn't peaches and
cream, but it was not the same coming
home to an empty bed. Ray and I were
no longer tight after what happened.
This was my choice. If he had it his
way, we would be together now. I
wasn't doing that. I needed to feel
the touch of a man. Not just any man
though. Some one that knew how I
deserve to be treated and that would

love my three kids unconditionally. I
knew that was a lot to ask for, but I
didn't deserve less.

I had a girl's night out with my
sister. Mom kept our kids. We went to
a movie and then to a late meal at
Chops. It was nice. It had been so
long since I was single that I forgot
how it felt to have heads turn when you
walk by and being able to flirt back.
We were average looking, but when we
got dressed we looked good.

"Girl, look at that man at the
table @ 5:00. He is checking you out."

"Is he cute?" I asked.

"Girl, if I wasn't married we
might be fighting now."

I turned around and she was right.
Not only was he fine but he was
checking me out. When I looked he
didn't even turn away. He smiled. He
had a different waitress than we did so
when I saw him talking to ours I wanted
to know what he was up to.

"Excuse me?" I said beckoning for
the waitress. "Can we have our check
now?"

"Well, that gentleman over there
has already taken care of your bill.
He also was waiting to see if you all
wanted something else," the waitress
said.

"Thank you," I said.

"Girl I dare you to go tell him
thank you," my sister said.

"You know that I am not shy at
all. I'll go," I declared getting up

from the table. I walked over to his
table where he sat alone and thanked
him. "I just came over to thank you
for dinner."

"You are more than welcome. I
couldn't believe that two beautiful
ladies were out eating alone and had no
one to pay for their meals. I couldn't
bear that thought so I handled it."

"We appreciate your kindness."

"What is your name?"

"My name is Melody and my
sister's…"

He interrupted, "No offense, but
your name was what I wanted. I believe
your sister is married, huh?" He asked.

"How do you know that?"

"Besides that big rock on her
finger I don't know. Are you married?"

"Not anymore."

"Don't be ashamed. Is this your
first time out since your divorce, or
do you and your entourage get together
often?"

"Shucks. This is my first time
out since my wedding day. Well, even
then I eloped."

"That's awful."

"We're about to go now. We have
to get our children from our mother's
house and then head home."

"Wait. My name is Al. Can I call
you sometime?"

"Sure."

I gave him my number and we left. I
hope I didn't seem too desperate. I
had never dated anyone besides Carl so

I was looking forward to Al's phone
call. He did call that night as a
matter of fact. We didn't talk long,
but long enough to set up a date. We
went out a few times, and I was hooked
on Al. I think he was just someone on
the rebound. He knew that I was hooked
too. By the next date he had me and I
mean all of me. Nothing compared to my
experience with Ray, but it was nice to
be treated like a queen.

"Are you all right?" he asked
holding me.

"I'm fine. I am eager to get in
the shower though," I said laughing.

"I have something to tell you."

"You better not tell me you got
AIDS or nothing."

"No. No. I should've told you
before, but I knew you wouldn't want to
see me again."

"What?"

"I am married."
My heart dropped. I was not thinking
of that bomb. "You wait until you get
me in bed to tell me this? Are you
joking? Have you bumped your head?"

"No, I wish I was. I am sorry."

"I really like you. How could you
do such a low down thing?"

"We are not happy. She has a
boyfriend too."

"So why not get a divorce or get
separated? Do you guys have kids?"

"We are just like roommates. We
have a daughter, but she doesn't know
what is going on."

"I'll bet she does. How old is she?"

"She's 12."

"She knows."

I continued seeing him despite his marriage. I believed that they were about to get divorced like he said. After a few months I called his house and she answered. I hung up. Why did I do that? That was the thing that I hated the most about Carl's girls. They'd hang up like teenagers. Look at me doing the same thing. I was no different than the woman or women that Carl was seeing. We decided to call it quits after a few more months. His wife actually called me. She told me that I was breaking up their home. She said that they had been happy until I came along. I don't know what he told her, but apparently she thinks it was one time affair and then Mr. Honesty felt compelled to confess because of his love for his family. I didn't tell her any different. He was lying to both of us. At least I knew that I was being lied to. She thought he was trying to do right. I was going on with my life from there.

From time to time I'd go to this little jazz club to listen to the music, and get a daiquiri or two. It reminded me of the scenes from the old movies with the little stage and round tables. One day I brought my sax and the guys actually let me sit in. I got a standing ovation. They wanted to give

me a set of my own on the weekends. I
would've taken it, but I found out that
I was pregnant again. I tried to reach
Al to let him know, but he wanted no
parts of it. My family knew about my
baby's daddy being Al, however they
didn't know that he was married. I had
so many skeletons in my closet. I felt
like the world's biggest whore. I kept
the baby of course and gave birth to a
beautiful baby girl named Amber Chenae
Frazier. I kept my married name after
my divorce. I went through so many
stages of depression after her birth.
I couldn't remember a happy time in my
life. All my mind could think of was
gloom. I didn't have the time to do
what I loved most, which was my music.
As I sat on my bed one night I decided
to play Amber a lullaby. As I was
playing I heard somebody say, "I am
married to the backslider." I dropped
my sax on the bed and ran to the other
room. No one was there. Then I heard
it three more times. I got my Bible
out of my trunk in my bedroom and
looked up backslider in the back of the
bible. It didn't have backslider but
backsliding. I went to Jeremiah
3:14,15 and it read: Turn, O
backsliding children, saith the LORD;
for I am married unto you: and I will
take you one of a city, and two of a
family, and I will bring you to Zion:
And I will give you pastors according
to mine heart, which shall feed you
with knowledge and understanding.

I broke down in tears. I knew that
I had to find my way back to God. That
was the only time that I was truly
happy. I got the yellow pages and I
prayed and told the Lord that I would
trust him to lead me to the church
where I could get what I needed. He
did just that. This church had a
strong youth ministry just like the one
I grew up in. Not only was the youth
ministry off of the hook, the singles
ministry was awesome too. The church
was actually praying for a Spirit-
filled saxophonist to record with them
on their next album, which was to be
recorded in the next few months.

I rededicated my life to the Lord
and my joy was restored. I got my
peace of mind back and a recording
contract to do a solo album. God is a
God that makes our dreams reality when
we serve Him.

Chapter Seven

DELORIS

My motto used to be "if you want it you can have it." I have been an optimistic person forever. Nothing is ever as bad as it seems. I have always seen the light at the end of the tunnel or the silver lining around the cloud. I could find a way to make the devil an angel. Let me tell it, in every bad situation there was some good in it. Once I got a taste of life my motto slightly changed to "be careful for what you ask for because you just may get it." A lot of times we are like children. All we see is the candy and the satisfaction our taste buds will get. Our parents see the stomachache and the rotten teeth that we could get. We still want what we want, when we want it, and how we want it. Sometimes in life we get what we want and end up throwing up, or having our teeth pulled. Like my mom says "if you make your bed hard you're the one that has to sleep in it." I didn't learn all of this until I became a mature adult. As a child I just overlooked obstacles and somehow I excelled in everything that I endeavored to do. According to others around me I had no reason to want to live, but my mom taught me to always

look for the good in others and myself.
She said I could do what anyone else
could do and that I was equal with
everybody else and that's what I
believed. My dad died in Vietnam and
that sent my mom into an early labor
with me. I was premature and had major
complications. I weighed only four
pounds, my lungs were underdeveloped,
and my left arm was on backwards. I
had to remain in the hospital for
months. Once I started breathing
normally they found complications with
my arm. It was twisted to the point
that I looked as if some one were
ringing out a towel. They couldn't
straiten it out so I ended up having it
amputated. My family treated me like I
was normal. No one acted as if I was
handicapped or special. All of my
cousins played the regular kid games
with me like hopscotch, hide and seek,
and even kick ball. It wasn't until I
went to public school that I realized
that I was different. I thought I was
as pretty as they came. People would
stop me and say "Oh you have such a
pretty face." As if having one arm
changed how I looked. I did everything
all humans did. I washed my body,
combed my dolls hair, I could write,
and I could even fight. One day these
girls were picking on me in the
bathroom.

"Look at the one armed soldier,"
one girl said. Everyone else was
laughing.

"Tag. You're it. Oh I forgot, how are you going to hit me back?" she said putting one of her arms in her sleeve.
She was running around tapping the other girls with her elbow and they were cheering her on with their laughter. Of course I saw no humor in what she was doing. It really hurt my feelings, but I refused to let them see me cry. It seemed to be what they wanted.

"Why exactly *are* you doing this?"

"Awe. Shut up handy girl. What exactly *are* you going to do about it? Are you going to hit me?"

"No. I am about to show the rest of my classmates how to ignore ignorance."

"I'll kick your butt. Who do you think you're talking to?"

"That's what I have been trying to figure out," I said as I walked toward the door of the rest room.

She ran up to me and said, "We gone see at lunchtime who I am."

I simply walked to class and proceeded as if nothing happened. I was petrified. I had no siblings and no relatives that attended my school. How was I going to fight her? One thing was for sure, I wasn't going to run from anyone. Even if she beats me up she will know that Deloris Dixon had been in battle with her. I had no appetite, but I ate anyway. I was taught to "let no one intimidate you

and not to intimidate people". I went
to play on the swing. There were a few
kids that didn't mind being with me.

"Uh…oh. Here comes trouble," one
classmate said. I didn't even look.

"Hey handy girl! How are you
holding on to the swing? Oh I see with
your invisible arm. Well I guess I
have to pull your other arm out and
shove it down your throat. Maybe then
you won't have so much mouth."

She pushed me off of the swing.
When she pushed me this sense of
strength came over me. I felt like I
grew ten feet. All I know is that I
grabbed her and hit her head against
the bar on the swing. As she fell I
kicked her got on top of her and
proceeded to slap her silly. The
teacher told me to get up, but my
adrenaline was pumping and I couldn't
get up. It took two teachers to get
little me off of that girl. Once it
was over I began to have an asthma
attack. I didn't have them frequently,
but when I did it was something
terrible. I felt like I was sinking in
a big tub of gel. It was as if my body
was filling up with the gel and once it
got to the top I blacked out. When I
came to myself I was coughing
uncontrollably to the point where I
started vomiting. I could hear the
people around me panicking. I blacked
out again. This time when I came to
doctors surrounded me. I was in the
hospital for three days and then I

returned home. I didn't go back to
school until that following Monday.
When I returned I had a fan club.
People were calling me "Little Sugar
Ray." Everybody wanted to sit with me
at lunch and it was all well with me.
I was never bullied again. My nickname
followed me through high school. Not
only was I bad in the ring, but I had
to be a tutor academically too. I kept
a grade point average of 4.0 at all
times. Some people still acted as if I
was a walking disease, but they kept
their comments to themselves or said
them in a way that I didn't know what
was being said.

During my senior year I won our
school talent show. I sang so well
that my music teacher convinced me to
try out for the "Search for the Stars"
auditions that were taking place in our
city. I did and I won. I would be
competing during the fall season after
graduation. I was so excited. My mom
and I flew to California for the
taping. The staring started as soon as
we got on the plane. It didn't hurt
because I felt that God had placed me
on this earth to make a difference and
if anyone had a reason to be ashamed it
was the people that thought that
something was wrong with me. The real
issue was with them. People didn't
like what they didn't understand. I
also hate when people try to make me
handicapped, but they too lacked
understanding. They are used to having

all of their limbs, but I functioned
better than they did. I surely had
more self-esteem than most women that I
came in contact with. I had such high
self-confidence that once people
started talking to me they ended asking
me for advice on how to build their
esteem. I even had the opportunity to
speak at high schools around my city.
I was determined to have everything I
wanted out of life and I got it too.

Once I won the competition I had
offers from two of the most popular
labels. I went with the one that had
the most popularity. Here I was beating
the odds. They wanted me to be a
charity case, but I was about to blow
up with fame and fortune. My
confidence shortly became arrogance and
the fans didn't like that. It's one
thing to be hated or mistreated in
school, but when your livelihood
depends on who likes you or not then
you have trouble. I grew big fast and
hard, but I fell bigger and harder. I
was broke before I knew it. I had a
few music award nominations, but didn't
win a thing. Back to South Carolina I
went.

I couldn't find a job that paid
what I wanted and didn't want to work
in the public eye I was embarrassed
because of how I had let everyone down
in my city. I decided to go to school.
I knew that I would succeed in that. I
wanted to be a teacher -- maybe I could
give back to the kids. During my days

in school I still encountered people
that wanted to make fun of me, but I
was a fighter and wasn't going to let
my peers faze me. We were there for
the same thing, and nine times out of
10, the one's that made fun needed my
help before it was over.

   I didn't date much, but I had my
share of men. Most guys had something
to prove to themselves, and I ended up
being their charity case. I wasn't
having that. I would rather be alone
than somebody's project. I went to
this revival at my cousin's church and
it was nice. The choir was
spectacular. They had about 25 people,
but they sounded 200 strong. The
organist mesmerized me -- he was
absolutely gorgeous. He played like an
angel. It was as if he could make the
organ talk. I had to meet him.

   "Girl, who is that man on the
organ?"

   "Shhhh… His name is Darnel.
Why?", my cousin asked.

   "I have got to meet him. Is he
married?"

   "No. You don't want to tread
those waters girl, believe me."

   "Is he our age?"

   "Yeah. Girl, listen to me. Leave
that alone."

   "Tara, you know me."

   "Yeah. I also know Darnel."

   "I still want to meet him."

"That is not the reason that you came to church anyway. I invited you here to meet another man, Jesus."

"Well, I don't want to hook up with Him. That is who I want to meet," I said pointing to the organist.

"Girl, you need to be saved."

"I am saved. I am just as saved as anyone else in here. Ain't nobody better than anyone else. My preacher says that no one that walked the earth is perfect but Jesus. So don't try that holy stuff with me."

"You still have to chose whether you want him as Lord of your life and then you live according to his Word not what you think. Never mind. One day you will realize that the only one that can make you complete is God."

"Until *then*?"

"Until then I will pray for your soul," she said and turned her head back to the preacher.

She was such a religious fanatic. Everything was Jesus, Jesus, and Jesus. It didn't take all of that. I had done much more charity work than she would ever have done. I was an honest person and I loved everybody. What more was there? After the service was over I walked over to the organ and introduced myself. When he saw me he almost exploded into laughter. He was very arrogant, but I was that much more determined to get with him. He was too much to let go. He must have never heard me sing. It didn't matter. This

man was going to fall for me. I told
him that I had to sing in a wedding and
I needed someone to play for me.

"I only play gospel music," he
said.

"That's fine. Let's try 'The
Lord's Prayer'."

"What key?"

"C sharp."

I began singing and he backed me
up oh too well. Somehow I had to get
this wedding cancelled, but keep my
connections with Darnel. Apparently I
wasn't the only one that wanted him. I
got all these ugly stares after I sang.
I knew that they were just jealous
because he was impressed with me. I
wanted to stick out my tongue at them,
but I was too classy for that.
Something in me said that he wasn't
interested in anything more than just a
friendship and possibly me singing with
the church, but I was going for the
gusto. I started coming to the church
regularly. I never joined, but they
let me sing constantly.

One day I asked Darnel to come
over for dinner and he accepted. I
made a simple dinner with spaghetti,
tossed salad; garlic bread, peach
cobbler, and homemade lemonade. He was
really impressed with my abilities to
cook.

"I am not trying to be funny but
did you cook all of this food by
yourself?"

"Yes I did. People think that I
am handicapped, but I manage to get
along better than folk with two arms."

"That's deep. When I first saw
you it caught me off guard when I
realized that you had only one arm."

"Yeah. I noticed when you had to
control your laughter. I overlooked it
though."

"I wasn't laughing at you. It was
more of a nervous laughter."

"Whatever. I am glad that you
enjoyed dinner. Are you ready for
dessert?"

"What's for dessert?"

"Peach cobbler and vanilla ice
cream. I made the cobbler, but I can't
take credit for the ice cream."

"So do you live here alone?"

"No. My mom lives here. She's
rarely here though. Her best friend
stays a couple of hours away. She has
cancer and my mom takes care of her
along with her nurse."

"Are you the only child?"

"Yes. When my dad died in Vietnam
my mom was pregnant with me and she
never remarried nor had other
children."

"What about a boyfriend?"

"Now you are getting personal. I
don't date on the regular because most
men try to make our relationship a
charity case. Like they are doing me a
favor by taking me out."

"It's not like you don't look
good. You are very attractive and you

have a very nice body. I guess it frightens people to see you with one arm. I not trying to be..."

"Don't feel like you need to apologize. I appreciate your honesty it's refreshing."

Once he said that it broke the ice. I started feeling comfortable with him. I even felt like if it went no further that it was all right. We talked, laughed, watched movies, and ate some more. He didn't leave until three the next morning. There was no hanky panky, just chilling with a friend.

He wanted to show me his skills in the kitchen so he invited me to his house, and he threw down. He had to show me up. He had candles every where with appetizers on the table, hot wings, celery, dip, and sweet tea. Then he brought out the main course of roast beef, scalloped potatoes, string beans, and corn bread. For dessert he made cheesecake with a chocolate crust and topping.

"Now I know you had this meal ordered from a restaurant. There is no way that a man can throw down like this."

"Girl, I know that you aren't stereotyping. We talked about that before. I can cook. I can do a lot of things that may shock you. Don't get me started."

"You really have a nice place do you live alone?"

"No. I have a roommate named Maurice."

"Where is he?"

"He works at night."

We talked the night away. I wanted to kiss him, but I was scared. I didn't want him to freak out. I wanted to be touched by him. Was I supposed to ask? I had only been intimate with one guy and it was a wham-bam, thank you ma'am. There was no foreplay, he just got what he wanted and he left. I could tell with the attention that he showed to his music, cooking, and his apartment that whatever he took time to be involved with he put his all into. I knew the heat that I felt in me, but was he on fire too? How would I know? We had already talked about relationships so I knew he didn't have a steady. He said he was a Christian. He didn't seem fanatical like my cousin. I didn't want to offend him but I can't take this any longer. I walked behind him and I started massaging his neck. He tensed up so much that I thought his neck would pop. I got afraid and I think he did too. I started to stop, but I was in the water too deep now. He eventually loosened up. From there I started kissing him on his neck. As I got around to his face I noticed that his eyes were closed. I knew I had him then. Once I got to his lips he took it from there. FIRE! He treated me like I was a Hammond b3 organ. He hit

keys that I didn't know existed. Round
and round we went. Every round went
higher and higher. This was one roller
coaster ride that didn't make me sick.
When it was over I knew it was over
between us. I was just glad that I got
what I wanted. I figured that he
wouldn't want to have anything else to
do with me after that happened. I
showered and went on to my house. When
I got home there was a message on my
answering machine.

"Hi. This is Darnel. I was just
calling to say that I really enjoyed
your company tonight. It was very
nice. I'll call you tomorrow. Maybe
you'll call me when you get in to let
me know that you're ok. Bye."

I couldn't believe he called me.
I couldn't wait to tell my cousin.

"Guess who I am seeing?"

"Mmm...Mmm...Mmm. You are a trip. I
hope that you are happy."

"Why don't you sound happy for me?
You have always been my ace. Why are
you tripping?"

"It ain't you boo. It's him.
I've known him for years and there has
been a lot of talk about him. I just
don't want you to get hurt. You are so
outgoing, but I wish you would hear me.
Just don't get too involved with him.
Please."

"Don't worry about me. Just be
happy for me. I might end up marrying
him."

"I really doubt that seriously. Darnel isn't the 'marrying' type."

"I guess time will tell this story. The Darnel you know may be a different one than the I know."

"I hope and pray so."

We saw each other almost everyday. He even took me to meet his mother. She was very pleasant. She was a big woman though. She was all of six feet tall and she had to weigh a good 300 pounds. She actually had my CD in her collection of music. She loved music and had the most beautifully soulful soprano voice. I was glad that we had a lot in common. He had a little sister too. She was about 12 years old. She was kind of frail looking, but she was cute for her age. She asked for my autograph like I was still a hot item on the market. There was one person in his life that acted like I was cool, but I could feel their resentment and that was Maurice, his roommate. If I came over he would speak and then leave the room and sometimes he left the house.

"What's up with Maurice? He never sticks around when I am around."

"He's like that. It is not you...well it doesn't matter. You're here to see me and not him. When I start acting weird then you can worry. Ok.?"

"Ok. I guess."

"Deloris. There is something I want to tell you and I hope you don't get offended."

"What is it?"

"Sit over here by me. I have had a lot of relationships and I want to be up front with you. Lately you have been the only person that I have been with. I want more than what we have in a relationship. I have had dates and one night stands over the years, but out of all of the people that I have been with I have never felt what I feel when I am with you. You have brought out feelings in me that I haven't felt in years, and I believe that you are the one for me. How do you feel about me?"

"I feel the same way. When I wake up in the morning you're the first thing on my mind and the last thing on my mind at night. I know that I love you."

"I know that I need you. I have done so many bad things in the past and I want to be honest with you," he said.

"Do you have any children?"

"No. I have had major issues in my life with relationships and I want to be real with this one."

"It would not be fair for me to question your past. I am just glad that you want to be so open. Let us just start from now. I guess that's what my cousin was talking about."

"What do you mean? What did she say?"

"She just warned me to be careful.
She didn't go into any detail, and I
didn't want to know."

"If we are going to get serious
about us then I have to totally commit
to God."

"Uh...oh. What do you mean?"

"I mean that in order for a
relationship or anything to be
successful God has to be the center of
it. I was born and raised in the
church and I know that I have to come
correct with God if I want his blessing
on my life. If you are planning to be
with me, He has to be the head of your
life too. It can't be because you want
to be with me either. It has to be
because you want to please Him. I
promised the Lord that if He ever
allowed me to feel whole again that I
would give him my all. Ever since we
have been serious I have felt like a
real man. You brought back something
that I prayed to get back, and I can't
go back on my vow to God."

"What am I suppose to do? I do
love the Lord. I am good. What more
do I need?"

"Being good isn't enough. He died
for our sins and accepting him as Ruler
of your life makes you whole. We
committed a crime through Adam and
Jesus took the blame. There was no one
on earth that was good enough to pay
for our crime so God came down in the
form of man and with His life paid our
ransom. All He wants in return is for

us to live like the Bible teaches.
First admit that you are a sinner then
repent for your sins. Secondly
acknowledge His virgin birth, death,
and resurrection from the dead and
believe it wholeheartedly. You would
then be considered a Christian. Then
it becomes a lifestyle. As you grow
you'll learn."

"Woe. You sound like a straight
up preacher. No one ever made it that
simple. My cousin is a fanatic. I
don't know how to do that. I don't
feel it like that. Now what you
described I can do. I feel like I owe
God or something."

"You and I both owe a debt we
could never repay and that's why we
give him control over our lives. Your
cousin is not a fanatic. She's just in
love with God and what He has done for
her. Once you develop a relationship
with Him you'll be a 'fanatic' too.
Watch and see."

We both got on our knees and he led us
in prayer. We were both crying like
babies. I gave my life to Christ. I
am saved. I never felt so free in my
life. It was awesome. In church he
stood and testified about what
happened. The whole church was
rejoicing. People were dancing and
praising God all over that church. Who
would've thought that my cousin and I
would be worshiping together through
Darnel witnessing to me? She told me
it didn't even matter who did the work

she was just glad that I was on the
Lord's side now.

A lot of people had a problem with
our relationship, but that didn't stop
us from witnessing to people and
bringing souls to Christ. People were
drawn to us. Once we got married we
really started ministering. He even
got ordained to be a minister in the
church. After a year he was offered to
be the pastor's assistant. I was right
by his side. After a few years of
diligently working in the church and
seeing people get delivered and saved
Darnel got really sick. The doctors
said that he had pneumonia. He stayed
in the hospital for weeks. He had this
horrible cough, he would break out into
sweats, and he was constantly throwing
up. He kept a fever and his room even
smelled like heat and sickness. He was
losing so much weight. He normally
weighed 190 and in a matter of weeks he
has withered to a measly 175. He was
so weak and he looked fragile. I was
scared to hold him too tight. We
prayed, but it seemed to just get
worse.

"Baby, I really need to talk to
you," he said one evening at the
hospital.

"What is it? I asked rubbing his
hand. His posture reminded me of that
night we gave our lives to the Lord.

"I need to tell you something. A
few years ago before we got married I
tried to tell you, but you said you

didn't want to know about my past. Now
I have to tell you. When I told you
that you had brought back feelings that
I hadn't had in a long time I was
sincere, but I wasn't direct. When I
was younger a relative molested me and
it really messed me up. I grew up
dating girls and even sleeping with
them, but I wanted men. Once I got to
be an adult I began to go both ways.
There were rumors out about me and most
were true. I always denied being
bisexual but I was. When we met things
changed. Since I have been with you
there have been no other men or women.
When I repented I gave all of that up.
However, the Word even teaches that
whatever you sow you are going to reap.
I sowed to my flesh and now I am
reaping. I have AIDS and I am going to
die. That's why I am not getting any
better. Unless God works a miracle I
will be dead this time next year. My
biggest concern was my soul and I have
been living totally for God these past
few years. Now my concern is you. You
know we have insurance and once I am
gone you will never have to worry about
anything financially. I am sorry you
had to find out like this."
 I was floored. I didn't speak for a
good 10 minutes. How could this happen
to me?
        "I don't know what to say. This
is just as much my fault as yours. I
never thought that you were gay or
bisexual. We have won so many souls to

Christ together. I was won to Christ
through you. If I had listened to my
cousin, I probably wouldn't be saved
now. I don't understand Darnel. Help
me understand. What are we going to
tell people? So many people look up to
you. What if they leave the Lord?
What if I have AIDS? I could die too?
What am I going to do? What are we
going to do? We are saved now. God
has to heal you. Maybe He will work a
miracle."

"I already have my answer from the
Lord and this is His will. He told me
that He had to use me as an example to
others like me that are faking it. He
must show the world that there is a
consequence to sin. The wages of sin
is still death. As long as I know that
my soul is right with Him I don't care
what others say or think. I just want
people to know that they have to be
real with God or this will happen. As
far as you are concerned I pray that
you use this as a stepping stone and
not a stumbling block. I pray that you
don't have this virus. It is possible
that you don't. You have to get tested
though. Don't waste time. Get tested
as soon as possible. Deloris, I do
love you and I never intended for this
to happen."

"I love you too. I had a chance
to not get involved with you, but I
chose to. We have to pay for our
choices sometimes. I pray that I don't
have it, but if I do I'll bow out

gracefully and I will share my
testimony to win other souls."
 We did more crying and hugging than
talking that night. I had so many
mixed emotions. I was sad that I would
soon be widowed. I was angry that I
hadn't listened to my cousin. I was
scared that I was going to die and I
was happy that I knew the Lord. The
only thing that kept me sane was the
Holy Ghost. I went that very next day
to be tested. The next week my doctor
let me know that my test came back
negative. I still had to go back in
six months to make sure. Once I went
back to the doctor for my six-month
test he told me that it was positive.
I was crushed, but I knew that it was
very likely. How could I have thought
differently? I knew that Darnel was
going to die, but I promised to never
remarry. I was not trying to spread an
epidemic. Instead I was going to try
to educate as many as I could about
this disease once I was thoroughly
taught. As I sat at that hospital with
Darnel I couldn't help but pray for a
miracle. I didn't want to be a widow
and I surely didn't want to die. I had
been at the hospital for 48 hours
straight. I was exhausted so I told
the doctor that I was going home for
the evening. I never told Darnel my
test results. I really didn't want to
bring him down anymore than he already
was. No sooner than I got home did I
get a call from the hospital saying

that I needed to get there as soon as
possible. When I got there they
wouldn't let me in. He has started
throwing up blood and passing blood
uncontrollably through his rectum. As
fate would have it my dear husband went
on home to be with the Lord. I can't
describe the emptiness that I felt
inside of me. Although I knew he was
going to die I could never prepare for
the grief that I experienced. I loved
him so much. He was the reason I came
to Christ.

We had his home going service
within a week of his death. I didn't
know that he knew so many people. Now
I know why Maurice didn't care for me.
He was one of his lovers. He never
told me, but the Lord did.

Darnel left me everything. He had
sole charge of his father's estate and
was still making money off of it. His
parents divorced when he was a kid, and
his dad never remarried. When he died
he willed everything he owned to his
heir Darnel. We also had a couple
hundred thousand in insurance on him.
After we paid for the funeral it all
came to me. No amount of money could
replace what we had and how much I
loved him. I decided to take this in
stride and do as I promised my husband
and that was to be a witness and a
testimony until the day that I died. I
was glad we didn't have children. That
would have made things a lot harder.
One thing I did know was that God has a

way getting glory from the tragedies in our lives. The devil meant it for bad but my Bible tells me that "all things work together for the good to them that love the Lord and are called according to his purpose." So when it is bad it is still good, and when it is good, it is good. There's no way to lose when you love the Lord. Now my motto is like the Apostle Paul says "to live is Christ and to die is gain."

Chapter Eight

KELLY, LYDIA, AND DIANE

We all had one thing in common. At one time or another we lived in the same house. A house is a place to dwell, and for most people, it is a place of refuge. For us, it was a place of torment. Although we stayed together for most of our lives, we hardly knew each other. I believed one of the reasons that we didn't become as close as we could've been is because we all shed light on something none of us wanted to face and that was the truth. The truth has a way of making you free and until you are ready to deal with it you stay in a fantasy world. My name is Kelly. I'd always been laid back. I didn't say much, but when I did talk there was something on my mind. As a child I had a lot of issues dealing with other children. I didn't like kids. I always wanted to be around adults. They were always into something good. They made their own rules and could do whatever they wanted to do with little or no consequences. I don't remember much of my childhood and what I do remember is a blur. I remember high school. That was when I began to grow. I began hanging out with the seniors. We would skip school and go get high or just chill out at one of our friend's houses. At the beginning we toyed with petty narcotics like marijuana. After a while we graduated to crack. That was the drug that would take me out of this hemisphere to somewhere else. When I was high Lydia somehow caught me. She really got on my nerves. She was almost like my mom.

"What are you doing out of school today, Kelly?" she asked.

"Taking care of my business and leaving yours alone."

"You don't have to get smart. I just know that you are hanging with the wrong crew and I really don't want you to get into any trouble."

"You are not that much older than I am. Why don't you just go away."

"I won't bother you now, but one day you'll need me."

"When pigs fly." I kind of liked the fact that someone cared because my mom didn't. Mom was an alcoholic and she left me alone years ago. I hardly even saw her. My friends were my family and we stuck together like glue. When I didn't see Lydia I missed her, but when she was around she made me feel guilty. One day my friend Patrick didn't have any rocks or weed, and we were in need of a serious high.

"I ain't got no money on me," I said.

"You are always broke Kelly. It's time for you to pay some dues. You be leaching off of us and it's time to pay the piper," Patrick said.

"I thought we were family, man," I said.

"And family help each other and we need your help."

"What am I supposed to do?"

"Let's walk up to the mall. We might be able to get some cheap jewelry or something," Dee-Dee said.

"We? I am not a thief. I don't steal girl -- are you crazy?"

"See you ain't been with us long enough. You ain't seen nothing. You have to go in 'cause they know us. All you have to do is go into the Woolworth and find some kind of jewelry that we can give Pookie 'nem. The biggest thing is you have to stay away from the camera. Act like you going to get some pads, go to the counter as if you 'bout to pay and say 'oh my God I left my purse in my car. I'll be right back.' That will distract the cashier. Put the stuff in your pocket and walk past the door and you're out," Dee-Dee said.

"You sound like you are a professional."

"You just have to know how to get what you need that's all," Patrick said.

We all would hang out at his house. After a few months, I just dropped out of school. I thought that school was for kids. Even though I was a kid, I didn't feel like it and I didn't have what most kids had,

parents. Other than Lydia, I had no
accountability. Shoplifting eventually
became what we did. I was scared each
time, but in order to survive I had to.
I had gotten so addicted to crack that
we started breaking into people's
houses.

There was this one pawnshop at the
corner of 155th and M. L. King, Jr. Ave.
that we had been checking out for a few
months. If we could get into that
joint, we would be set for a while.
Everybody that had ever tried to rob
them got caught. A couple of people
got shot. One day I was tore up, and
Patrick and me had it out. I left and
went walking and who did I run into?
Lydia.

"How you doing these days Kelly?"
she said.

"Heck I don't know. Why do you
always come around when I feel like
this?"

"Like what?"

"Just leave me alone."

"I did the last time you asked me,
but I won't this time. Why did you
stop going to school?"

"Look, you don't know me like
that. How do you know that I am not in
school? You ain't my Momma."

"Maybe I'm not, but there are a
lot of things I know about you that you
don't think any one else knows."

"Name one thing you know besides
the fact that you think I quit school."

"I know that you do drugs. As a matter of fact you are high right now."

"You are scaring me. Get away from me."

"Don't run Kelly let me help you!"

"You are the one that needs help. Quit following me!"

"Just let me help you."

"No! Stay away from me."

I went back but Patrick and Dee-Dee were gone. I sat on the step waiting for what seemed to be an eternity when I saw this beautiful lady walk up to me. What did she want?

"Why are you hanging with those thugs? You are better than that," she said.

"Excuse me whoever you are, those thugs are my family."

"Well, I can offer you much more than they could ever offer you. And you surely wouldn't have to live in this rat hole."

"If you have so much to offer what are you doing over here in this neighborhood? And why are you walking and not driving?"

"For you information I did drive. My car is up the street. I've been checking out this street for a while and I noticed you some time ago, I just wanted to give you a chance to get out of here and have some real fun."

"There're a lot people trying to help me." I mumbled under my breath.

"Excuse me?"

"Nothing. What ever you're offering I am not interested."

"OK. It's your choice."

I watched her walk out of my sight and curiosity was killing me. By the time she was gone Patrick and Dee-Dee were back.

"What's up with you staring all into space like you're messed up?" Dee-Dee asked.

"It's nothing. Just thought I saw someone I knew that's all. Where have you guys been?"

"Doing what you won't with your sorry tail," Patrick said going into the house.

"Look Pat, I can't risk robbing that pawn shop on MLK. No one has successfully robbed it, and I just can't get caught and go to jail."

"Kelly, we are in this together. If one go down, we all go down. That's just how it is. If you can't hang then you may just need to step off. Go hang with someone else."

"I don't have nobody else. Just y'all."

"Either you down or you not. If you are not with us you're against us and there's no need of you even being here. You may dime us out."

"I'd never do that."

"All I know is that we have been catching your slack and you have to do your part. Ain't no free lunch here."

"Dee-Dee you feel me don't you, girl?" I asked.

"I feel you but Patrick is right.
I have to do my part too. It's a risk
for me just like it is for you."

"Man, this ain't right. I'll be
back."

"Where are you going?" Dee-Dee
asked.

"I just have to think some things
over that's all."
I left and went walking up the street
looking for that lady. Maybe she could
help me make some money and I wouldn't
have to steal. That way Patrick and
Dee-Dee would not keep pressuring me.
I couldn't go to jail. I saw the lady
about to get into a car almost a block
off.

"Wait. Wait. What's up? What's
the deal for real?"

"Come with me."

We got into this big black
Cadillac. She had a driver and
everything. The mere fact that she was
out that time of night gave me the
impression that whatever she did wasn't
that much more legal than what I was
already doing.

"I have girls that work for me. I
have my own house, and that's where
they work. We only service certain
people, and I protect all the girls.
By the way my name is Diane. I am
protected by another source, but what
do you have to lose. We charge
according to what the customers want."

"You are a female pimp?"

"No. I am a Madame. I take care of my girls. They are clean and tested regularly for sexually transmitted diseases and AIDS. I don't fight to get my money it's almost like a room and board situation. Condoms are always worn."

"Like I said you're a female pimp. I am not any whore. I have never even slept with any man for that matter. I am only 17."

"Girl, I start 'em way younger than you. See whores are on the street. I have saved my girls from the streets and that's why they are so loyal to me. I know you be getting high and that's cool too. We got what ever you need, and you don't have to steal a thing. Just shake your moneymaker and be creative and you are in the house baby. I got somebody that will break you in if you want him to. It'll be worth it. After he's done you can begin training. We have movies and plenty of experienced girls there that will help you get orientated."

"OK."

"Everybody is shaky at first, but before you know it you will be one of my trainers."

We drove up to this big pretty white house. It looked like a plantation. Diane had land as far as the eye could see. They treated me like gold. I was led to my room and I was instructed by one of "the girls" to

get showered and changed. They had
lingerie for me.

"My name is Sugar, and if you have
any questions you can feel free to ask
me anything."

"Do I have to wear this? I asked
lifting up a teddy.

"Yes. Do you not like that
color?"

"It's not that. I am not used to
wearing … you know."

"I was nervous when I first came
too. We don't wear clothes around here
much. That's part of the job. We are
like family, but we don't mix business
with pleasure. Well, yes we do. Our
job is pleasure. This is who you are
now. We don't use our real names
because that is not who you are
anymore. We belong to Diane and her
rules flow here. She doesn't ask for
much, but you have to provide the
fantasy. That's what keeps business
booming. You'll get used to it. I
hear you are fresh meat, huh?"

"What, do you mean a virgin?"

"Yes," she said.

"Yes I am."

"You are in for a treat honey.
Big daddy handles the fresh meat. You
don't have a thing to be worried about.
He's a great butcher."

"Butcher, no thanks. I'm
leaving."

"He's not a real butcher. Put it
this way. Out of all of the men that
come through here, the girls request to

see him again and again. Once you're
broken in you're not allowed to see him
in that way anymore. So you might want
to take your time getting adjusted to
getting laid because once he says you
are ready you go to the next level."

"What's that?"

"Screwing for money and not for
your pleasure but theirs. That is the
only thing that I hate. Some men want
to see you enjoy yourself, but most men
just want to get off. That's what we
do. I have a cute name for you."

"What?"

"Luscious. Do you like it?"

"I guess. It sure does sound
seductive."

"Once you're broken in you start
off at the bottom. That's new men and
cheap guys. Once you start getting
requests then you move up. That's when
you go to the other house. It's behind
this one. That's where the VIPs are.
We get politicians, celebrities, even
preachers are up in here."

"You are lying."

"I am afraid not. We are well
known for our service, and Diane don't
play."

"Who is she seeing?"

"She doesn't share her secrets,
but she doesn't do what we do."

"Isn't this illegal?"

"Girl, just like drugs, sex sales.
Who's gonna bust us? When you service
the people that could arrest you or
convict you, you don't worry."

"This is a trip. What do I do once I get showered and dressed? Or should I say undressed?"

"Go to your phone and dial 3 and I will take you to Big Daddy."

"Can I dial out?"

"No. We have to use the pay phone down stairs. That's another safety precaution. Most of us here don't have anyone on the outside to call. Do you?"

"My family Dee-Dee and Patrick. We went to school together. We dropped out together. We got high together. I didn't get to say bye. I fought with Patrick and met Diane within an hour of each other. They are going to be worried about me."

"The only thing I can suggest is that you write them. You can't give them a return address other than getting the P.O. box from Diane. Chances are that won't happen until she knows you well. At least they'll know you're all right if you write them."

That is what I planned to do while I was on break if we got them. Once I got ready she took me to Big Daddy's suite. It looked like something out of a movie. He had a kitchen, bedroom, study, and the room for "business". That room was connected to the bathroom.

"Aren't you some pretty fresh meat? What's your name sweetie?"

"Kelly. Sugar says that she
wanted to change it to Luscious but
Kelly is just fine thank you."
He was already smoking weed. He had
incense burning, and it seemed like I
was in a horror movie. I wanted to run
out of there, but I knew there was no
turning back once I'd gone this far. I
thought that he would be some old
perverted looking man. He was far from
that. Miss Diane had good taste in men
and in everything I had seen so far. I
still had to get used to the idea of
being a whore. They call it being an
escort, but I knew the real deal.
People had a way of making the wrong
they do sound right some how.

"Sit down and relax. You can keep
on your robe until you are ready to
take it off. I am in no hurry. I
don't rush to do anything. As a matter
of fact until I say you are ready you
don't go any further."

"So what if I am never ready?"

"After a few hours or days of
being with me you will be ready. You
probably won't want to leave. All we
have here is time," he said smiling.

This man was some one to want. He
had to be all of six feet, four inches
and 220 pounds. He was light brown and
he had the prettiest teeth. Diane did
make it easy for me. We talked,
smoked, drank, and tripped out at some
dirty movies. It still took me a
couple of days before I let him take my
only prized possession. I always

thought that my first time would be
with a man that I was in love with, but
at least I can act like we are in love.
Although we weren't in love he still
was sensitive to the fact that I
thought that this should be special.
He didn't make me do anything that I
didn't want to. He started kissing me
and I started crying.

"I have done this a few times, but
I have never had anyone cry on me.
What's wrong?"

"I have never done this before and
I am scared. I thought that this would
be something that I would share with
someone that I was in love with."

"Do you have a good imagination?"

"I guess."

"Just lay back and listen to the
music. Do you want me to put on some
other type of music?"

"No. This is pretty." The music
was soulful but it sounded classical
too.

"Relax. Listen to the music and
imagine that you're at the place that
you would want to be and with the
person that you want to be with," he
said as he began kissing me. I
imagined that he was my husband and
this was our wedding night. He had
provided me with all of the other
fantasy that I needed. As pain turned
into pleasure, I just held on and
waited for the ride to slow down so
that I could start over again. Big
Daddy was the only one that made

history in my life. I would never
forget how he made such an unfavorable
situation exceptionally wonderful.
I saw what Sugar was talking about.
When it was time to go, I was not
ready. I hadn't seen Diane in a few
days, but I heard that that was normal.
Once I got the hang of things, I moved
up really quickly. I actually had one
of my teachers from high school as a
client. You would be surprised at the
traffic that came through there. I
became Diane's favorite. I had so many
requests that they had to put some on a
waiting list. Most men got turned
away. After about three years of sex,
drugs, booze, and money I got really
sick. It was like my body was breaking
down. One night I almost overdosed and
they had to take me to the emergency
room. After the doctors ran tests, of
course they found drugs, but I also had
gonorrhea and a bladder infection. I
had been unprotected a few times with a
couple of regulars and it caught up
with me. I couldn't find Diane
anywhere.

"How did I get here?"

"Ma'am you were left outside no one
brought you here." The nurse said.

I had no number to call and no
address to report to. I had no family,
nothing. What was I supposed to do?
My memory was so shot that I could
hardly remember what I did yesterday
let alone where I stayed. We were
sequestered and had no reason to leave.

Diane was the ruler of my world and now she was gone. I looked up and who did I see but Lydia. Now wasn't that a blimp.

"I told you that you couldn't get away from me," she said.

"How did you know that I was here. I haven't seen you in years. This is impossible."

"No. It is fate. I have come to rescue you. Seeing how you have no one else I believe this time you will let me help you."

"You can't help me."

"Kelly. Do you want help?"

"Yes," I said and then broke down and cried.

"We have to first start by being honest with ourselves."

"I don't know how. I don't know who I am."

"That's the best start, honesty," she said holding me.

"I am going crazy."

"No. No. Once you get better here, I have a clergyman that I have been telling to pray for you for the longest. Especially after I couldn't find you. He said if I ever found you that we could meet with him and he would give free counseling. I will set up an appointment and I'll even go with you. Please let me do this for you. For us."

"Ok."

Before I got out of the hospital, the minister and Lydia were at my bedside.

"I know that this may be hard for you, but you have to be honest with yourself first and then with me. My name is Reverend Jacobs. I am a licensed psychologist as well and I have been sent to help you. Do you understand what I am saying to you?"

"Yes."

"Do you mind me recording this session although it is informal?"

"No. You can record."

"Before we start let's pray." He prayed for about a minute and then proceeded. "Let's start with you stating your full name," he said.

"My name is Kelly..."

"Uh...remember you have to be honest with yourself before I can be of any help to you."

"My name is Lydia Nicole Reid."

"Good. Now, tell me about Kelly and Diane."

"Kelly is who I am when I want to get high."

"Do you want to stop?"

"No," I said wiping my face. "She made me feel all right with being on drugs. Diane is the part of me that made it cool to be a prostitute. I felt if I had permission to do it that I was still a good person. Big Daddy was my pimp. Prostitution was the only way that I could support my habit. Although I stayed in an abandoned building Diane made it luxurious for me. I didn't want to face Patrick and Dee-Dee being a whore and all, so

that's why I left them. I still don't
know how I got here but I just want to
be better. Kelly hated Lydia because
that is who she really was. We all
shared the same house, but not at the
same time. Now that I know that I need
help Lydia is ready to come out. I
want to get rid of Kelly and Diane, but
I don't know how. Please help me."
During that session the Rev. Dr. Jacobs
introduced me to Christ. Once I fully
came to myself I realized that I was on
the floor for the mentally insane.
Once I was treated for my sicknesses,
they took me to this floor because I
was talking to myself and it seemed to
me that there were people there. At
first I was there for evaluation, but
by the time Kelly and Lydia were done,
I was committed. At the second
session, the Rev. Dr. Jacobs put oil on
my head and laid hands on me. After I
got off of the floor, I never had a
taste for drugs or alcohol again. It
is hospital policy that before a mental
patient is released that they are
evaluated for at least six months to a
year. God worked on my behalf so that
they released me within two months.
Now I am working side by side with the
Rev. Dr. and have been for the past
five years. I am clean and sober. I
am currently seeking funding for my
support group, which is headed by the
doctor, but run by another former
addict and me. We are seeking funding
to get a shelter for young girls that

are prostituting their bodies for money. We will help them and drug users get clean, get jobs, and obtain housing. I can now say that I was once a prostitute, a drug addict, an alcoholic, and I suffered with multiple personalities disorder, but now I am a born again believer. I have been washed in the blood of the Lamb. I can now say I once was lost but now I am found. I was blind, but thank God, now I see. What can wash away my sins? Nothing but the blood of Jesus. What can make me whole again? Nothing but the blood of Jesus.

The End

This book was sponsored by:

Universal Outreach Ministries
P.O. Box 2503
Stone Mountain, GA 30086

ISBN 141200263-X